"I Conquered"

By HAROLD TITUS

With Frontispiece in Colors
By CHARLES M. RUSSELL

A. L. BURT COMPANY
Publishers   New York

Published by Arrangements with RAND, MCNALLY & COMPANY

Copyright, 1916,
By RAND McNALLY & COMPANY

Printing Statement:

Due to the very old age and scarcity of this book, many of the pages may be hard to read due to the blurring of the original text, possible missing pages, missing text, dark backgrounds and other issues beyond our control.

Because this is such an important and rare work, we believe it is best to reproduce this book regardless of its original condition.

Thank you for your understanding.

THE CONTENTS

CHAPTER		PAGE
I.	Denunciation	7
II.	A Young Man Goes West	21
III.	"I've Done My Pickin'"	36
IV.	The Trouble Hunter	48
V.	Jed Philosophizes	62
VI.	Ambition Is Born	74
VII.	With Hoof and Tooth	89
VIII.	A Head of Yellow Hair	98
IX.	Pursuit	106
X.	Capture	120
XI.	A Letter and a Narrative	131
XII.	Woman Wants	141
XIII.	VB Fights	151
XIV.	The Schoolhouse Dance	163
XV.	Murder	181
XVI.	The Candle Burns	192
XVII.	Great Moments	201
XVIII.	The Lie	214
XIX.	Through the Night	226
XX.	The Last Stand	235
XXI.	Guns Crash	245
XXII.	Tables Turn; and Turn Again	254
XXIII.	Life, the Trophy	265
XXIV.	Victory	276
XXV.	"The Light!"	290
XXVI.	To the Victor	297

"— I CONQUERED"

CHAPTER I

DENUNCIATION

DANNY LENOX wanted a drink. The desire came to him suddenly as he stood looking down at the river, burnished by bright young day. It broke in on his lazy contemplation, wiped out the indulgent smile, and made the young face serious, purposeful, as though mighty consequence depended on satisfying the urge that had just come up within him.

He was the sort of chap to whom nothing much had ever mattered, whose face generally bore that kindly, contented smile. His grave consideration had been aroused by only a scant variety of happenings from the time of a pampered childhood up through the gamut of bubbling boyhood, prep school, university, polo, clubs, and a growing popularity with a numerous clan until he had approached a state of established and widely recognized worthlessness.

Economics did not bother him. It mattered not how lavishly he spent; there had always been more forthcoming, because Lenox senior had a world of the stuff. The driver of his taxicab —

just now whirling away — seemed surprised when Danny waved back change, but the boy did not bother himself with thought of the bill he had handed over.

Nor did habits which overrode established procedure for men cause him to class himself apart from the mass. He remarked that the cars zipping past between him and the high river embankment were stragglers in the morning flight businessward; but he recognized no difference between himself and those who scooted toward town, intent on the furtherance of serious ends.

What might be said or thought about his obvious deviation from beaten, respected paths was only an added impulse to keep smiling with careless amiability. It might be commented on behind fans in drawing rooms or through mouths full of food in servants' halls, he knew. But it did not matter.

However — something mattered. He wanted a drink.

And it was this thought that drove away the smile and set the lines of his face into seriousness, that sent him up the broad walk with swinging, decisive stride, his eyes glittering, his lips taking moisture from a quick-moving tongue. He needed a drink!

Danny entered the Lenox home up there on the sightly knoll, fashioned from chill-white stone, staring composedly down on the drive from its many black-rimmed windows. The heavy front door shut behind him with a muffled sound like a sigh, as though it had been waiting his coming all through the night, just as it had through so many nights, and let suppressed breath slip out in relief at another return.

A quick step carried him across the vestibule within sight of the dining-room doorway. He flung his soft hat in the general direction of a cathedral bench, loosed the carelessly arranged bow tie, and with an impatient jerk unbuttoned the soft shirt at his full throat. Of all things, from conventions to collars, Danny detested those which bound. And just now his throat seemed to be swelling quickly, to be pulsing; and already the glands of his mouth responded to the thought of that which was on the buffet in a glass decanter — amber — and clear — and —

At the end of the hallway a door stood open, and Danny's glance, passing into the room it disclosed, lighted on the figure of a man stooping over a great expanse of table, fumbling with papers — fumbling a bit slowly, as with age, the boy remarked even in the flash of a second his mind required to register a recognition of his father.

Danny stopped. The yearning of his throat, the call of his tightening nerves, lost potency for the moment; the glitter of desire in his dark eyes softened quickly. He threw back his handsome head with a gesture of affection that was almost girlish, in spite of its muscular strength, and the smile came back, softer, more indulgent.

His brow clouded a scant instant when he turned to look into the dining room as he walked down the long, dark, high-ceilinged hall, and his step hesitated. But he put the impulse off, going on, with shoulders thrown back, rubbing his palms together as though wholesomely happy.

So he passed into the library.

"Well, father, it's a good morning to you!"

At the spontaneous salutation the older man merely ceased moving an instant. He remained bent over the table, one hand arrested in the act of reaching for a document. It was as though he held his breath to listen — or to calculate quickly.

The son walked across to him, approaching from behind, and dropped a hand on the stooping, black-clothed shoulder.

"How go —"

Danny broke his query abruptly, for the other straightened with a half-spoken word that was, at the least, utmost impatience; possibly a word which, fully uttered, would have expressed disgust, perhaps — even loathing! And on Danny was turned such a mask as he had never seen before. The cleanly shaven face was dark. The cold blue eyes flashed a chill fire and the grim slit of a tightly closed mouth twitched, as did the fingers at the skirts of the immaculate coat.

Lenox senior backed away, putting out a hand

to the table, edging along until a corner of it was between himself and his heir. Then the hand, fingers stiffly extended, pressed against the table top. It trembled.

The boy flushed, then smiled, then sobered. On the thought of what seemed to him the certain answer to the strangeness of this reception, his voice broke the stillness, filled with solicitude.

"Did I startle you?" he asked, and a smile broke through his concern. "You jumped as though —"

Again he broke short. His father's right hand, palm outward, was raised toward him and moved quickly from side to side. That gesture meant silence! Danny had seen it used twice before — once when a man of political power had let his angered talk rise in the Lenox house until it became disquieting; once when a man came there to plead. And the gesture on those occasions had carried the same quiet, ominous conviction that it now impressed on Danny.

The voice of the old man was cold and hard, almost brittle for lack of feeling.

"How much will you take to go?" he asked, and breathed twice loudly, as though struggling to hold back a bursting emotion.

Danny leaned slightly forward from his hips and wrinkled his face in his inability to understand.

"What?" He drawled out the word. "Once more, please?"

"How much will you take to go?"

Again the crackling, colorless query, by its chill strength narrowing even the thought which must transpire in the presence of the speaker.

"How much will I take to go?" repeated Danny. "How much what? To go where?"

Lenox senior blinked, and his face darkened. His voice lost some of its edge, became a trifle muffled, as though the emotion he had breathed hard to suppress had come up into his throat and adhered gummily to the words.

"How much money — how much money will you take to go away from here? Away from me? Away from New York? Out of my sight — out of my way?"

Once more the fingers pressed the table top and the fighting jaw of the gray-haired man protruded slowly as the younger drew nearer a faltering step, two — three, until he found support against the table.

There across the corner of the heavy piece of furniture they peered at each other; one in silent, mighty rage; the other with eyes widening, quick, confusing lights playing across their depths as he strove to refuse the understanding.

"How much money — to go away from New York — from you? Out of your *way?*"

Young Danny's voice rose in pitch at each word as with added realization the strain on his emotions increased. His body sagged forward and the hands on the table bore much of its weight; so much that the elbows threatened to give, as had his knees.

"To go away — why? Why — is this?'

In his query was something of the terror of a frightened child; in his eyes something of the look of a wounded beast.

"You ask me why!"

Lenox senior straightened with a jerk and followed the exclamation with something that had been a laugh until, driven through the rage within him, it became only a rattling rasp in his throat.

"You ask me why!" he repeated. "You ask me why!"

His voice dropped to a thin whisper; then, anger carrying it above its normal tone:

"You stand here in this room, your face like suet from months and years of debauchery, your mind unable to catch my idea because of the poison you have forced on it, because of the stultifying thoughts you have let occupy it, because of the ruthless manner in which you have wasted its powers of preception, of judgment, and ask me why!"

In quick gesture he leveled a vibrating finger at the face of his son and with pauses between the words declared: "*You* — are — why!"

Danny's elbows bent still more under the weight on them, and his lips worked as he tried to force a dry throat through the motions of swallowing. On his face was reflected just one emotion — surprise. It was not rage, not resentment, not shame, not fear — just surprise.

He was utterly confused by the abruptness of his father's attack; he was unable to plumb the depths of its significance, although an inherent knowledge of the other's moods told him that he faced disaster.

Then the older man was saying:

"You have stripped yourself of everything that God and man could give you. You have thrown the gems of your opportunity before your swinish desires. You have degenerated from the son your mother bore to a worthless, ambitionless, idealless, thoughtless — drunkard!"

Danny took a half-step closer to the table, his eyes held on those others with mechanical fixity.

"Father — but, dad —" he tried to protest.

Again the upraised, commanding palm.

"I have stood it as long as I can. I have suggested from time to time that you give serious consideration to things about you and to your future; suggested, when a normal young man would have gone ahead of his own volition to meet the exigencies every individual must face sooner or later.

"But you would have none of it! From your boyhood you have been a waster. I hoped once that all the trouble you gave us was evidence of a spirit that would later be directed toward a good end. But I was never justified in that.

"You wasted your university career. Why, you weren't even a good athlete! You managed to graduate, but only to befog what little hope then remained to me.

"You have had everything you could want; you had money, friends, and your family name. What have you done? Wasted them! You had your polo string and the ability to play a great game, but what came of it? You'd rather sit in the clubhouse and saturate yourself with drink and with the idle, parasitic thoughts of the crowd there!

"You have dropped low and lower until, everything else gone, you are now wasting the last thing that belongs to you, the fundamental thing in life — your vitality!

"Oh, don't try to protest! Those sacks under your eyes! Your shoulders aren't as straight as they were a year ago; you don't think as quickly as you did when making a pretense of playing polo; your hand isn't steady for a man of twenty-five. You're going; you're on the toboggan slide.

"You have wasted yourself, flung yourself away, and not one act or thought of your experience has been worth the candle! Now — what will you take to get out?"

The boy before him moved a slow step backward, and a flush came up over his drawn face.

"You — " he began. Then he stopped and drew a hand across his eyes, beginning the movement slowly and ending with a savage jerk. "You never said a word before! You never intimated you thought this! You never — you —"

He floundered heavily under the stinging conviction that of such was his only defense!

"No!" snapped his father, after waiting for more to come. "I never said anything before — not like this. You smiled away whatever I suggested. Nothing mattered — nothing except debauchery. Now you've passed the limit You're a common drunk!"

His voice rose high and higher; he commenced to gesticulate.

"You live only to wreck yourself. Yours is the fault — and the blame!

"It is natural for me to be concerned. I' e hung on now too long, hoping that you would right yourself and justify the hopes people have had in you. I planned, years ago, to have you take up my work where I must soon leave off — to go on in my place, to finish my life for me as I began yours for you! I've had faith that you would do this, but you won't — you can't!

"That isn't all. You're holding *me* back. I must push on now harder than ever, but with the stench of your misdeeds always in my nostrils it is almost an impossibility."

Danny raised his hands in a half-gesture of pleading, but the old man motioned him back.

"Don't be sorry; don't try to explain. This had to come. It's an accumulation of years.

I have no more faith in you. If I thought you could ever rally I'd give up everything and help you, but not once in your life have you shown me that you possessed one impulse to be of use."

His voice dropped with each word, and its return to the cold normal sent a stiffness into the boy's spine. His head went up, his chin out; his hands closed slowly.

"How much money will you take to get out?"

The old man moved from behind the table corner and approached Danny, walking slowly, with his hands behind him. He came to a stop before the boy, slowly unbuttoned his coat, reached to an inner pocket, and drew out a checkbook.

"How much?"

Danny's gesture, carried out, surely would have resulted in a blow strong enough to send the book spinning across the room; but he stopped it halfway.

His eyes were puffed and bloodshot; his pulse hammered loudly under his ears, and the rush of blood made his head roar. Before him floated a mist, fogging thought as it did his vision.

The boy's voice was scarcely recognizable as he spoke. It was hard and cold — somewhat like the one which had so scourged him.

"Keep your money," he said, looking squarely at his father at the cost of a peculiar, unreal effort. "I'll get out — and without your help. Some day I'll — I'll show you what a puny thing this faith of yours is!"

The elder Lenox, buttoning his coat with brisk motions, merely said, "Very well." He left the room.

Danny heard his footsteps cross the hall, heard the big front door sigh when it closed as though it rejoiced at the completion of a distasteful task.

Then he shut his eyes and struck his thighs twice with stiff forearms. He was boiling, blood and brain! At first he thought it anger; perhaps anger had been there, but it was not the chief factor of that tumult.

It was humiliation. The horrid, unanswerable truth had seared Danny's very body — witness the anguished wrinkles on his brow — and his molten consciousness could find no argument to justify himself, even to act as a balm!

"He never *said* it before," the boy moaned, and in that spoken thought was the nearest thing to comfort that he could conjure.

He stood in the library a long time, gradually cooling, gradually nursing the bitterness that grew up in the midst of conflicting impulses. The look in his eyes changed from bewilderment to a glassy cynicism, and he began to walk back and forth unsteadily.

He paced the long length of the room a dozen times. Then, with a quickened stride, he passed into the hall, crossed it, and entered the dining room, the tip of his tongue caressing his lips.

On the buffet stood a decanter, a heavy affair

of finely executed glassworker's art. The dark stuff in it extended halfway up the neck, and as he reached for it Danny's lips parted. He lifted the receptacle and clutched at a whisky glass that stood on the same tray. He picked it up, looked calculatingly at it, set it down, and picked up a *tumbler*.

The glass stopper of the bottle thudded on the mahogany; his nervous hand held the tumbler under its gurgling mouth. Half full, two-thirds, three-quarters, to within a finger's breadth of the top he filled it.

Then, setting the decanter down, he lifted the glass to look through the amber at the morning light; his breath quick, his eyes glittering, Danny Lenox poised. A smile played about his eager lips — a smile that brightened, and lingered, and faded — and died.

The hand holding the glass trembled, then was still; trembled again, so severely that it spilled some of the liquor; came gradually down from its upraised position, down below his mouth, below his shoulder, and waveringly sought the buffet.

As the glass settled to the firm wood Danny's shoulders slacked forward and his head drooped. He turned slowly from the buffet, the aroma of whisky strong in his dilated nostrils. After the first faltering step he faced about, gazed at his reflection in the mirror, and said aloud:

"And it's not been worth — the candle!"

Savagery was in his step as he entered the

hall, snatched up his hat, and strode to the door.

As the heavy portal swung shut behind the hurrying boy it sighed again, as though hopelessly. The future seemed hopeless for Danny. He had gone out to face a powerful foe.

CHAPTER II

A Young Man Goes West

FROM the upper four hundreds on Riverside Drive to Broadway where the lower thirties slash through is a long walk. Danny Lenox walked it this June day. As he left the house his stride was long and nervously eager, but before he covered many blocks his gait moderated and the going took hours.

Physical fatigue did not slow down his progress. The demands upon his mental machinery retarded his going. He needed time to think, to plan, to bring order out of the chaos into which he had been plunged. Danny had suddenly found that many things in life are to be considered seriously. An hour ago they could have been numbered on his fingers; now they were legion. It was a newly recognized fact, but one so suddenly obvious that the tardiness of his realization became of portentous significance.

Through all the hurt and shame and rage the great truth that his father had hammered home became crystal clear. He had been merely a waster, and a sharp bitterness was in him as he strode along, hands deep in pockets.

The first flash of his resentment had given birth to the childish desire to "show 'em," and as he crowded his brain against the host of strange facts he found this impulse becoming stronger, growing into a healthy determination to adjust his standard of values so that he could, even with this beginning, justify his existence.

Oh, the will to do was strong in his heart, but about it was a clammy, oppressive something. He wondered at it — then traced it back directly to the place in his throat that cried out for quenching. As he approached a familiar haunt that urge became more insistent and the palms of his hands commenced to sweat. He crossed the street and made on down the other side. He had wasted his ability to do, had let this desire sap his will. He needed every jot of strength now. He would begin at the bottom and call back that frittered vitality. He shut his teeth together and doggedly stuck his head forward just a trifle.

The boy had no plan; there had not been time to become so specific. His whole philosophy had been stood on its head with bewildering suddenness. He knew, though, that the first thing to do was to cut his environment, to get away, off anywhere, to a place where he could build anew. The idea of getting away associated itself with one thing in his mind: means of transportation. So, when his eyes without conscious motive stared at the poster advertising a railroad system that crosses the continent, Danny

Lenox stopped and let the crowd surge past him.

A man behind the counter approached the tall, broad-shouldered chap who fumbled in his pockets and dumped out their contents. He looked with a whimsical smile at the stuff produced: handkerchiefs, pocket-knife, gold pencil, tobacco pouch, watch, cigarette case, a couple of hat checks, opened letters, and all through it money — money in bills and in coins.

The operation completed, Danny commenced picking out the money. He tossed the crumpled bills together in a pile and stacked the coins. That done, he swept up the rest of his property, crammed it into his coat pockets, and commenced smoothing the bills.

The other man, meanwhile, stood and smiled.

"Cleaning up a bit?" he asked.

Danny raised his eyes.

"That's the idea," he said soberly. "To clean up — a bit."

The seriousness of his own voice actually startled him.

"How far will that take me over your line?" he asked, indicating the money.

The man stared hard; then smiled.

"You mean you want that much worth of ticket?"

"Yes, ticket and berth — upper berth. Less this." He took out a ten-dollar bill. "I'll eat on the way," he explained gravely.

The other counted the bills, turning them over with the eraser end of his pencil, then counted the silver and made a note of the total.

"Which way — by St. Louis or Chicago?" he asked. "We can send you through either place."

Danny lifted a dollar from the stack on the counter and flipped it in the air. Catching it, he looked at the side which came up and said:

"St. Louis."

Again the clerk calculated, referring to time-tables and a map.

"Denver," he muttered, as though to himself. Then to Danny: "Out of Denver I can give you the Union Pacific, Denver and Rio Grande, or Santa Fé."

"The middle course."

"All right — D. and R.G."

Then more referring to maps and time-tables, more figuring, more glances at the pile of money.

"Let's see — that will land you at — at —" as he ran his finger down the tabulation — "at Colt, Colorado."

Danny moved along the counter to the glass-covered map, a new interest in his face.

"Where's that — Colt, Colorado?" he asked, leaning his elbows on the counter.

"See?" The other indicated with his pencil. "You go south from Denver to Colorado Springs; then on through Pueblo, through the Royal Gorge here, and right in here —" he put the lead point down on the red line of the railroad and Danny's head came close to his — "is where you get off."

The boy gazed lingeringly at the white dot in the red line and then looked up to meet the other's smile.

"Mountains and more mountains," he said with no hint of lightness. "That's a long way from this place."

He gazed out on to flowing Broadway with a look somewhat akin to pleading, and heard the man mutter: "Yes, beyond easy walking from downtown, at least."

Danny straightened and sighed. That much was settled. He was going to Colt, Colorado. He looked back at the map again, possessed with an uneasy foreboding.

Colt, Colorado!

"Well, when can I leave?" he asked, as he commenced putting his property back into the proper pockets.

"You can scarcely catch the next train," said the clerk, glancing at the clock, "because it leaves the Grand Central in nineteen min —"

"Yes, I can!" broke in Danny. "Get me a ticket and I'll get there!" Then, as though to himself, but still in the normal speaking tone: "I'm through putting things off."

Eighteen and three-quarters minutes later a tall, young man trotted through the Grand Central train shed to where his Pullman waited.

The porter looked at the length of the ticket Danny handed the conductor.

"Ain't y'll carryin' nothin', boss?" he asked.

"Yes, George," Danny muttered as he passed into the vestibule, "but nothing you can help me with."

With the grinding of the car wheels under him Danny's mind commenced going round and round his knotty problem. His plan had called for nothing more than a start. And now — Colt, Colorado!

Behind him he was leaving everything of which he was certain, sordid though it might be. He was going into the unknown, ignorant of his own capabilities, realizing only that he was weak. He thought of those burned bridges, of the uncertainty that lay ahead, of the tumbling of the old temple about his ears —

And doubt came up from the ache in his throat, from the call of his nerves. He had not had a drink since early last evening. He needed — No! That was the last thing he needed.

He sat erect in his seat with the determination and strove to fight down the demands which his wasting had made so steely strong. He felt for his cigarette case. It was empty, but the tobacco pouch held a supply, and as he walked toward the smoking compartment he dusted some of the weed into a rice paper.

Danny pushed aside the curtain to enter, and a fat man bumped him with a violent jolt.

"Oh, excuse me!" he begged, backing off. "Sorry. I'll be back in a jiffy with more substantial apologies."

Three others in the compartment made room for Danny, who lighted his cigarette and drew a great gasp of smoke into his lungs.

In a moment the fat man was back, his eyes dancing. In his hand was a silver whisky flask.

"Now if you don't say this is the finest booze ever turned out of a gin mill, I'll go plumb!" he declared. "Drink, friend, drink!"

He handed the flask to one of the others.

"Here's to you!" the man saluted, raising the flask high and then putting its neck to his mouth.

Danny's tongue went again to his lips; his breath quickened and the light in his eyes became a greedy glitter. He could hear the gurgle of the liquid; his own throat responded in movement as he watched the swallowing. He squeezed his cigarette until the thin paper burst and the tobacco sifted out.

"Great!" declared the man with a sigh as he lowered the flask. "Great!"

He smacked his lips and winked. "Ah! No whisky's bad, but this's better'n most of it!"

Then, extending the flask toward Danny, he said: "Try it, brother; it's good for a soul."

But Danny, rising to his feet with a suddenness that was almost a spring, strode past him to the door. His face suddenly had become tight and white and harried. He paused at the entry, holding the curtain aside, and turned to see the other, flask still extended, staring at him in bewilderment.

"I'm not drinking, you know," said Danny weakly, "not drinking."

Then he went out, and the fat man who had produced the liquor said soberly:

"Not drinking, and havin' a time staying off it. But say — ain't that some booze?"

Long disuse of the power to plan concretely, to think seriously of serious facts, had left it weak. Danny strove to route himself through to that new life he knew was so necessary, but he could not call back the ability of tense thinking with a word or a wish. And while he tried for that end the boy commenced to realize that perhaps he had not so far to seek for his fresh start. Perhaps it was not waiting for him in Colt, Colorado. Perhaps it was right here in his throat, in his nerves. Perhaps the creature in him was not a thing to be cleared away before he could begin to fight — perhaps it was the proper object at which to direct his whole attack.

Enforced idleness was an added handicap. Physical activity would have made the beginning much easier, for before he realized it Danny was in the thick of battle. A system that had been stimulated by poison in increasing proportion to its years almost from boyhood began to make unequivocal demands for the stuff that had held it to high pitch. Tantalizingly at first, with the thirsting throat and jumping muscles; then with thundering assertions that warped the vision and numbed the intellect and toyed with the will. He gave up trying to think ahead. His entire mental force went into the grapple with that desire. Where he had thought to find possible distress in the land out yonder, it had come to meet him — and of a sort more fearful, more tremendous, than any which he had been able to conceive.

Through the rise of that fevered fighting the words of his father rang constantly in Danny's mind.

"He was right — right, right!" the boy declared over and over. "It was brutal; but he was right! I've wasted, I've gone the limit. And he does n't think I can come back!"

While faith would have been as a helping hand stretched down to pull him upward, the denial of it served as a stinging goad, driving him on. A chord deep within him had been touched by the raining blows from his father, and the vibrations of that chord became quicker and sharper as the battle crescendoed. The unbelief had stirred a retaliating determination.

It was this that sent a growl of defiance into Danny's throat at sight of a whisky sign; it was the cause of his cursing when, walking up and down a station platform at a stop, he saw men in the buffet car lift glasses to their lips and smile at one other. It was this that drew him away from an unfinished meal in the diner when a man across the table ordered liquor and Danny's eyes ached for the sight of it, his nostrils begged for the smell.

So on every hand came the suggestions that made demands upon his resistance, that made the weakness gnaw the harder at his will. But he fought against it, on and on across a country, out into the mountains, toward the end of his ride.

The unfolding of the marvels of a continent's vitals had a peculiar effect on Danny.

Before that trip he had held the vaguest notions of the West, but with the realization of the grandeur of it all he was torn between a glorified inspiration and a suffocating sense of his own smallness.

He had known only cities, and cities are, by comparison, such puny things. They froth and ferment and clatter and clang and boast, and yet they are merely flecks, despoiled spots, on an expanse so vast that it seems utterly unconscious of their presence. The boy realized this as the big cities were left behind, as the stretches between stations became longer, the towns more flimsy, newer. A species of terror filled him as he gazed moodily from his Pullman window out across that panorama to the north. Why, he could see as far as to the Canadian boundary, it seemed! On and on, rising gently, ever flowing, never ending, went the prairie. Here and there a fence; now a string of telephone poles marching out sturdily, bravely, to reduce distance by countless hours. There a house, alone, unshaded, with a woman standing in the door watching his speeding train. Yonder a man shacking along on a rough little horse, head down, listless — a crawling jot under that endless sky.

Even his train, thing of steel and steam, was such a paltry particle, screaming to a heaven that heard not, driving at a distance that cared not.

Then the mountains!

Danny awoke in Denver, to step from his car and look at noble Evans raising its craggy, hoary head into the salmon pink of morning, defiant, ignoring men who fussed and puttered down there in its eternal shadow; at Long's Peak, piercing the sky as though striving to be away from humans; at Pike, shimmering proudly through its sixty miles of crystal distance, taking a heavy, giant delight in watching beings worry their way through its hundred-mile dooryard.

Then along the foothills the train tore with the might of which men are so proud; yet it only crawled past those mountains.

Stock country now, more and more cattle in sight. Blasé, white-faced Herefords lifted their heads momentarily toward the cars. They heeded little more than did the mountains.

Then, to the right and into the ranges, twisting,

turning, climbing, sliding through the narrow defiles at the grace of the towering heights which — so alive did they seem — could have whiffed out that thing, those lives, by a mere stirring on their complacent bases.

And Danny commenced to draw parallels. Just as his life had been artificial, so had his environment. Manhattan — and this! Its complaining cars, its popping pavements, its echoing buildings — it had all seemed so big, so great, so mighty! And yet it was merely a little mud village, the work of a prattling child, as compared with this country. The subway, backed by its millions in bonds, planned by constructive genius, executed by master minds, a thing to write into the history of all time, was a mole-passage compared to this gorge! The Woolworth, labor of years, girders mined on Superior, stones quarried elsewhere, concrete, tiling, cables, woods, all manner of fixtures contributed by continents; donkey engines puffing, petulant whistles screaming, men of a dozen tongues crawling and worming and dying for it; a nation standing agape at its ivory and gold attainments! And what was it? Put it down here and it would be lost in the rolling of the prairie as it swelled upward to meet honest heights!

No wonder Danny Lenox felt inconsequential. And yet he sensed a friendly something in that grandeur, an element which reached down for him like a helping hand and offered to draw him out of his cramped, mean little life and put him up with stalwart men.

"If this rotten carcass of mine, with its dry throat and fluttering hands, will only stick by me I'll show 'em yet!" he declared, and held up one of those hands to watch its uncertainty.

And in the midst of one of those bitter, griping struggles to keep his vagrant mind from running into vinous paths, the brakes clamped down and the porter, superlatively polite, announced:

"This is Colt, sah."

A quick interest fired Danny. He hurried to the platform, stood on the lowest step, and watched the little clump of buildings swell to natural size. He reached into his pocket, grasped the few coins remaining there, and gave them to the colored boy.

The train stopped with a jolt, and Danny stepped off. The conductor, who had dropped off from the first coach as it passed the station, ran out of the depot, waved his hand, and the grind of wheels commenced again.

As the last car passed, Danny Lenox stared at it, and for many minutes his gaze followed its departure. After it had disappeared around the distant curve he retained a picture of the white-clad servant, leaning forward and pouring some liquid from a bottle.

The roar of the cars died to a murmur, a muttering, and was swallowed in the cañon. The sun beat down on the squat, green depot and cinder platform, sending the quivering heat rays back to distort the outlines of objects. Everywhere was a white, blinding light.

From behind came a sound of waters, and Danny turned about to gaze far down into a ragged gorge where a river tumbled and protested through the rocky way.

Beyond the stream was stretching mesa, quiet and flat and smooth looking in the crystal distance, dotted with pine, shimmering under the heat.

For five minutes he stared almost stupidly at that grand sweep of still country, failing to comprehend the fact of arrival. Then he walked to the end of the little station and gazed up at the town.

A dozen buildings with false fronts, some painted, some without pretense of such nicety, faced one another across a thoroughfare four times as wide as Broadway. Sleeping saddle ponies stood, each with a hip slumped and nose low to the yellow ground. A scattering of houses with their clumps of outbuildings and fenced areas straggled off behind the stores.

Scraggly, struggling pine stood here and there among the rocks, but shade was scant.

Behind the station were acres of stock pens, with high and unpainted fences. Desolation! Desolation supreme!

Danny felt a sickening, a revulsion. But lo! his eyes, lifting blindly for hope, for comfort, found the thing which raised him above the depression of the rude little town.

A string of cliffs, ranging in color from the bright pink of the nearest to the soft violet of those which might be ten or a hundred miles away, stretched in mighty columns, their varied pigments telling of the magnificent distances to which they reached. All were plastered up against a sky so blue that it seemed thick, and as though the color must soon begin to drip. Glory! The majesty of the earth's ragged crust, the exquisite harmony of that glorified gaudiness! Danny pulled a great chestful of the rare air into his lungs. He threw up his arms in a little gesture that indicated an acceptance of things as they were, and in his mind flickered the question:

"The beginning — or the end?"

CHAPTER III

"I'VE DONE MY PICKIN'"

THEN he felt his gaze drawn away from those vague, alluring distances. It was one of those pulls which psychologists have failed to explain with any great clarity; but every human being recognizes them. Danny followed the impulse.

He had not seen the figure squatting there on his spurs at the shady end of the little depot, for he had been looking off to the north. But as he yielded to the urge he knew its source — in those other eyes.

The figure was that of a little man, and his doubled-up position seemed to make his frame even more diminutive. The huge white angora chaps, the scarlet kerchief about his neck and against the blue of his shirt, the immense spread of his hat, his drooping gray mustache, all emphasized his littleness.

Yet Danny saw none of those things. He looked straight into the blue eyes squinting up at him — eyes deep and comprehensive, set in a copper-colored face, surrounded by an intricate design of wrinkles in the clear skin; eyes that had looked at incalculably distant horizons for decades, and had learned to look at men with that same long-range gaze. A light was in those eyes — a warm, kindly, human light — that attracted and held and created an atmosphere of stability; it seemed as though that light were tangible, something to which a man could tie — so prompt is the flash from man to man that makes for friendship and devotion; and to Danny there came a sudden comfort. That was why he did not notice the other things about the little man. That was why he wanted to talk.

"Good morning," he said.

" 'Mornin'."

Then a pause, while their eyes still held one another.

After a moment Danny looked away. He had a stabbing idea that the little man was reading him with that penetrating gaze. The look was kindly, sincere, yet — and perhaps because of it — the boy cringed.

The man stirred and spat.

"To be sure, things kind of quiet down when th' train quits this place," he remarked with a nasal twang.

"Yes, indeed. I — I don't suppose much happens here — except trains."

Danny smiled feebly. He took his hat off and wiped the brow on which beads of sweat glistened against the pallor. The little man still looked up, and as he watched Danny's weak, uncertain movements the light in his eyes changed.

The smile left them, but the kindliness did not go; a concern came, and a tenderness.

Still, when he spoke his nasal voice was as it had been before.

"Take it you just got in?"

"Yes — just now.'

Then another silence, while Danny hung his head as he felt those searching eyes boring through him.

"Long trip this hot weather, ain't it?"

"Yes, very long."

Danny looked quickly at his interrogator then and asked:

"How did you know?"

"Did n't. Just guessed." He chuckled.

"Ever think how many men's been thought wise just guessin'?"

But Danny caught the evasion. He looked down at his clothes, wrinkled, but still crying aloud of his East.

"I suppose," he muttered, "I do look different — *am* different."

And the association of ideas took him across the stretches to Manhattan, to the life that was, to —

He caught his breath sharply. The call of his throat was maddening!

The little man had risen and, with thumbs hooked in his chap belt, stumped on his high boot heels close to Danny. A curious expression softened the lines of his face, making it seem queerly out of harmony with his garb.

"You lookin' for somebody?" he ventured, and the nasal quality of his voice seemed to be mellowed, seemed to invite, to compel confidence.

"Looking for somebody?"

Danny, only half consciously, repeated the query. Then, throwing his head back and following that range of flat tops off to the north, he muttered: "Yes, looking for somebody — looking for myself!"

The other shifted his chew, reached for his hat brim, and pulled it lower.

"No baggage?" he asked. "To be sure, an' ain't you got no grip?"

Danny looked at him quickly again, and, meeting the honest query in that face, seeing the spark there which meant sympathy and understanding — qualities which human beings can recognize anywhere and to which they respond unhesitatingly — he smiled wanly.

"Grip?" he asked, and paused. "Grip? Not the sign of one! That's what I'm here for — in Colt, Colorado — to get a fresh grip!" After a moment he extended an indicating finger and asked: "Is that all of Colt — Colt, Colorado?"

The old man did not follow the pointing farther than the uncertain finger. And when he answered his eyes had changed again, changed to searching, ferreting points that ran over every puff and seam and hollow in young Danny's face. Then the older man set his chin firmly, as though a grim conclusion had been reached.

"That's th' total o' Colt," he answered. "It ain't exactly astoundin', is it?"

Danny shook his head slowly.

"Not exactly," he agreed. "Let's go up and look it over."

An amused curiosity drove out some of the misery that had been in his pallid countenance.

"Sure, come along an' inspect our metropolis!" invited the little man, and they struck off through the sagebrush.

Danny's long, free stride made the other hustle, and the contrast between them was great; the one tall and broad and athletic of poise in spite of the shoulders, which were not back to their full degree of squareness; the other, short and bowlegged and muscle-bound by years in the saddle, taking two steps to his pacemaker's one.

They attracted attention as they neared the store buildings. A man in riding garb came to the door of a primitive clothing establishment, looked, stepped back, and emerged once more. A moment later two others joined him, and they stared frankly at Danny and his companion.

A man on horseback swung out into the broad street, and as he rode away from them turned in his saddle to look at the pair. A woman ran down the post-office steps and halted her hurried progress for a lingering glance at Danny. The boy noticed it all.

"I'm attracting attention," he said to the little man, and smiled as though embarrassed.

"Aw, these squashies ain't got no manners," the other apologized. "They set out in these dog-gone hills an' look down badger holes so much that they git *loco* when somethin' new comes along."

Then he stopped, for the tall stranger was not beside him. He looked around. His companion was standing still, lips parted, fingers working slowly. He was gazing at the front of the Monarch saloon.

From within came the sound of an upraised voice. Then another in laughter. The swinging doors opened, and a man lounged out. After him, ever so faint, but insidiously strong and compelling, came an odor!

For a moment, a decade, a generation — time does not matter when a man chokes back temptation to save himself — Danny stood in the yellow street, under the white sunlight, making his feet remain where they were. They would have hurried him on, compelling him to follow those fumes to their source, to push aside the flapping doors and take his throat to the place where that burning spot could be cooled.

In Colt, Colorado! It had been before him all the way, and now he could not be quit of its physical presence! But though his will wavered, it held his feet where they were, because it was stiffened by the dawning knowledge that his battle had only commenced; that the struggle during the long journey across country had been only preliminary maneuvering, only the mobilizing of his forces.

When he moved to face the little Westerner his eyes were filmed. The other drew a hand across his mouth calculatingly and jerked his hat-brim still lower.

"As I was sayin'," he went on a bit awkwardly as they resumed their walk, "these folks ain't got much manners, but they're good hearted."

Danny did not hear. He was casting around for more resources, more reserves to reinforce his front in the battle that was raging.

He looked about quickly, a bit wildly, searching for some object, some idea to engage his thoughts, to divert his mind from that insistent calling. His eyes spelled out the heralding of food stuffs. The sun stood high. It was time. It was not an excuse; it was a Godsend!

"Let's eat," he said abruptly. "I'm starving."

"That's a sound idee," agreed the other, and they turned toward the restaurant, a flat-roofed building of rough lumber. A baby was playing in the dirt before the door and a chained coyote puppy watched them from the shelter of a corner.

On the threshold Danny stopped, confusion possessing him He stammered a moment, tried to smile, and then muttered:

"Guess I'd better wait a little. It is n't necessary to eat right away, anyhow."

He stepped back from the doorway with its smells of cooking food and the other followed him quickly, blue eyes under brows that now drew down in determination.

"Look here, boy," the man said, stepping close, "you was crazy for chuck a minute ago, an' now you make a bad excuse not to eat. To be sure, it ain't none of my business, but I'm old enough to be your daddy; I ain't afraid to ask you what's wrong. Why don't you want to eat?"

The sincerity of it, the unalloyed interest that precluded any hint of prying or sordid curiosity, went home to Danny and he said simply:

"I'm broke."

"You did n't need to tell me. I knowed it. I ain't, though. You eat with me."

"I can't! I can't do that!"

"Expect to starve, I s'pose?"

"No — not exactly. That is," he hastened to say, "not if I'm worth my keep. I came out here to — to get busy and take care of myself. I'll strike a job of some sort — anything, I don't care what it is or where it takes me. When I'm ready to work, I'll eat. I ought to get work right away, ought n't I?"

In his voice was a sudden pleading born of the fear awakened by his realization of absolute helplessness, as though he looked for assurance to strengthen his feeble hopes, but hardly dared expect it. The little man looked him over gravely from the heels of his flat shoes to the crown of his rakishly soft hat. He pushed his Stetson far back on his gray hair.

"To be sure, and I guess you won't have to look far for work," he said. "I've been combin' this town dry for a hand all day. If you'd like to take a chance workin' for me I'd be mighty glad to take you on — right off. I'm only waitin' to find a man — can't go home till I do. Consider yourself hired!"

He turned on his heel and started off. But Danny did not follow. He felt distrust; he thought the kindness of the other was going too far; he suspected charity.

"Come on!" the man snapped, turning to look at the loitering Danny. "Have I got to rope an' drag you to grub?"

"But — you see it's — this way," the boy stammered. "Do you really want me? Can I do your work? How do you know I'm worth even a meal?"

A slow grin spread over the Westerner's countenance.

"Friend," he drawled in his high, nasal tone, "it's a pretty poor polecat of a man who ain't worth a meal; an' it's a pretty poor specimen who goes hirin' without makin' up his mind sufficient. They ain't many jobs in this country, but just now they's fewer men. We've got used to bein' careful pickers. I've done my pickin'. Come on."

Only half willingly the boy followed.

They walked through the restaurant, the old man saluting the lone individual who presided over the place, which was kitchen and dining room in one.

"Hello, Jed," the proprietor cried, waving a fork. "How's things?"

"Finer 'n frog's hair!" the other replied, shoving open the broken screen door at the rear.

"This is where we abolute," he remarked, indicating the dirty wash-basin, the soap which needed a boiling out itself, and the discouraged, service-stiffened towel.

Danny looked dubiously at the array. He had never seen as bad, to say nothing of having used such; but the man with him sloshed water into the basin from a tin pail and said:

"You're next, son, you're next."

And Danny plunged his bared wrists into the water. It was good, it was cool; and he forgot the dirty receptacle in the satisfaction that came with drenching his aching head and dashing the cooling water over his throat. The other stood and watched, his eyes busy, his face reflecting the rapid workings of his mind.

They settled in hard-bottomed, uncertain-legged chairs, and Jed — whoever he might be, Danny thought, as he remembered the name — gave their order to the man, who was, among other things, waiter and cook.

"Make it two sirloins," he said; "one well done an' one —" He lifted his eyebrows at Danny.

"Rare," the boy said.

"An' some light bread an' a pie," concluded the employer-host.

Danny saw that the cook wore a scarf around his neck and down his back, knotted in three places. When he moved on the floor it was evident that he wore riding boots. On his wrists were the leather cuffs of the cowboy.

Danny smiled. A far cry, indeed, this restaurant in Colt, Colorado, from his old haunts along the dark thoroughfare that is misnamed a lighted way! The other was talking: "We'll leave soon's we're through an' make it on up th' road to-night. It'll take us four days to get to th' ranch, probably, an' we might's well commence. Can you ride?"

Danny checked a short affirmative answer on his lips.

"I've ridden considerably," he said. "You people wouldn't call it riding, though. You'll have to teach me."

"Well, that's a good beginnin'. To be sure it is. Them as has opinions is mighty hard to teach —'cause opinions is like as not to be dead wrong."

He smeared butter on a piece of bread and poked it into his mouth. Then:

"I brought out my last hand — I come with him, I mean. Th' sheriff brought him. His saddle an' bed's over to th' stable. You can use 'em."

"Sheriff?" asked Danny. "Get into trouble?"

"Oh, a little. He's a good boy, mostly — except when he gets drinkin'."

Danny shoved his thumb down against the tines of the steel fork he held until they bent to uselessness.

CHAPTER IV

The Trouble Hunter

KNEE to knee, at a shacking trot, they rode out into the glory of big places, two horses before them bearing the light burden of a Westerner's bed.

"My name's Jed Avery," the little man broke in when they were clear of the town. "I'm located over on Red Mountain — a hundred an' thirty miles from here. I run horses — th' VB stuff. They call me Jed — or Old VB; mostly Jed now, 'cause th' fellers who used to ca'l me Old VB has got past talkin' so you can hear 'em, or else has moved out. Names don't matter, anyhow. It ain't a big outfit, but I have a good time runnin' it. Top hands get thirty-five a month."

Danny felt that there was occasion for answer of some sort. In those few words Avery had given him as much information as he could need, and had given it freely, not as though he expected to open a way for the satisfaction of any curiosity. He wanted to forget the past, to leave it entirely behind him; did not want so much as a remnant to cling to him in this new life. Still, he did not deem it quite courteous to let the volunteered information come to him and respond with merely an acknowledgment.

He cleared his throat. "I'm from Riverside Drive, New York City," he said grimly. "Names *don't* matter. I don't know how to do a thing except waste time — and strength. If you'll give me a chance, I'll get to be a top hand."

An interval of silence followed.

"I never heard of th' street you mention. I know New York's on th' other slope an' considerable different from this here country. Gettin' to be a top hand's mostly in makin' up your mind — just like gettin' anywhere else."

Then more wordless travel. Behind them Colt dwindled to a bright blotch. The road ran close against the hills, which rose abruptly and in scarred beauty. The way was ever upward, and as they progressed more of the country beyond the river spread out to their view, mesas and mountains stretching away to infinite distance, it seemed.

Even back of the sounds of their travel the magnificent silence impressed itself. It was weird to Danny Lenox, unlike anything his traffic-hardened ears had ever experienced, and it made him uneasy—it, and the ache in his throat.

That ache seemed to be the last real thing left about him, anyhow. Events had come with such unreasonable rapidity in those last few days that his harassed mind could not properly arrange the impressions. Here he was, hired out to do he knew not what, starting a journey that would take him a hundred and thirty miles from a place called Colt, in the state of Colorado, through a country as unknown to him as the regions of mythology, beside a man whose like he had never seen before, traveling in a fashion that on his native Manhattan had worn itself to disuse two generations ago!

Out of the whimsical reverie he came with a jolt. Following the twisting road, coming toward them at good speed, was the last thing he would have associated with this place — an automobile. He reined his horse out of the path, saw the full-figured driver throw up his arm in salutation to Jed, and heard Jed shout an answering greeting. The driver looked keenly at Danny as he passed, and touched his broad hat.

"Who was that?" the boy asked, as he again fell in beside his companion.

"That's Bob Thorpe," the other explained. "He's th' biggest owner in this part of Colorado — mebby in th' whole state. Cattle. S Bar S mostly, but he owns a lot of brands."

"Can he get around through these mountains in a car?"

"He seems to. An' his daughter! My! To be sure, she'd drive that dog-gone bus right up th' side of that cliff! You'll see for yourself. She'll be home 'fore long — college — East somewheres."

The boy looked at him questioningly but said nothing. "College — East — home 'fore long —" Might it not form a link between this new and that old — a peculiar sort of link — as peculiar as this sudden, unwarranted interest in this girl?

Through the long afternoon Danny eagerly awaited the coming of more events, more distractions. When they came — such as informative bursts from Jed or the passing of the automobile — he forgot for the brief passage of time the throb in his throat, that wailing of the creature in him. But when the two rode on at the shambling trot, with the silence and the immense grandeur all about them, the demands of his appetite were made anew, intensified perhaps by a feeling of his own inconsequence, by the knowledge that should he fail once in standing off those assaults it would mean only another beginning, and harder by far than this one he was experiencing.

Every hour of sober reflection, of sordid struggle, added to his estimate of the strength of that self he must subdue. He was going away into the waste places, and a sneaking fear of being removed from the stuff that had kept him keyed commenced to grow, adding to the fleshly wants.

If he should be whipped and a surrender be forced? What then? He realized that that doubting was cowardice. He had come out here to have freedom, a new beginning, and now he found himself begging for a way back should the opposition be too great. It was sheer weakness!

Cautiously Jed Avery had watched Danny's

face, and when he saw anxiety show there as doubt rose, he broke into words:

"Yes, sir, Charley was sure a good boy, but th' booze got him."

He looked down at his horse's withers so he could not see the start this assertion gave Danny.

"He did n't want to be bad, but it's so easy to let go. To be sure, it is. Anyhow, Charley never had a chance, never a look-in. He was good hearted an' meant well — but he did n't have th' backbone."

And Danny found that a rage commenced to rise within him, a rage which drove back those queries that had made him weak.

Day waned. The sun slid down behind the string of cliffs which stretched on before them at their left. Distances took on their purple veils, a canopy of virgin silver spread above the earth, and the stillness became more intense.

"Right on here a bit now we'll stop," Jed said. "This 's th' Anchor Ranch. They're hayin', an' full up. We'll get somethin' to eat, though, an' feed for th' ponies. Then we'll sleep on th' ground. Ever do it?"

"Never."

"Well, you've got somethin' comin', then. With a sky for a roof a man gets close to whatever he calls his God — an' to himself. Some fellers out here never seem to see th' point. Funny. I been sleepin' out, off an' on, for longer than I like to think about — an' they's a feelin' about it that don't come from nothin' else in th' world."

"You think it's a good thing, then, for a man to get close to himself?"

"To be sure I do."

"What if he's trying to get away from himself?"

Jed tugged at his mustache while the horses took a dozen strides. Then he said:

"That ain't right. When a man thinks he wants to get away from himself, that's th' coyote in him talkin'. Then he wants to get closer'n ever; get down close an' fight again' that streak what's come into him an' got around his heart. Wants to get down an' fight like sin!"

He whispered the last words. Then, before Danny could form an answer, he said, a trifle gruffly:

"Open th' gate. I'll ride on an' turn th' horses back."

They entered the inclosure and rode on toward a clump of buildings a half-mile back from the road.

Off to their right ran a strip of flat, cleared land. It was dotted with new haystacks, and beyond them they could see waving grass that remained to be cut. At the corral the two dismounted, Danny stiffly and with necessary deliberation. As they commenced unsaddling, a trio of hatless men, bearing evidences of a strenuous day's labor, came from the door of one of the log houses to talk with Jed. That is, they came ostensibly to talk with Jed; in reality, they came to look at the Easterner wno fumbled awkwardly with his cinch.

Danny looked at them, one after the other, then resumed his work. Soon a new voice came to his ears, speaking to Avery. He noticed that where the little man's greeting to the others had been full-hearted and buoyant, it was now curt, almost unkind.

Curious, Danny looked up again — looked up to meet a leer from a pair of eyes that appeared to be only half opened; green eyes, surrounded by inflamed lids, under protruding brows that boasted but little hair, above high, sunburned cheek bones; eyes that reflected all the small meanness that lived in the thin lips and short chin. As he looked, the eyes leered more ominously. Then the man spoke:

"Long ways from home, ain't you?"

Although he looked directly at Danny, although he put the question to him and to him alone, the boy pretended to misunderstand — chose to do so because in the counter question he could express a little of the quick contempt, the instinctive loathing that sprang up for this man who needed not to speak to show his crude, unreasoning, militant dislike for the stranger, and whose words only gave vent to the spirit of the bully.

"Are you speaking to me?" Danny asked, and the cool simplicity of his expression carried its weight to those who stood waiting to hear his answer.

The other grinned, his mouth twisting at an angle.

"Who else round here'd be far from home?" he asked.

Danny turned to Jed.

"How far is it?" he asked.

"A hundred an' ten," Jed answered, a swift pleasure lighting his serious face.

Danny turned back to his questioner.

"I'm a hundred and ten miles from home," he said with the same simplicity, and lifted the saddle from his horse's back.

It was the sort of clash that mankind the world over recognizes. No angry word was spoken, no hostile movement made. But the spirit behind it could not be misunderstood.

The man turned away with a forced laugh which showed his confusion. He had been worsted, he knew. The smiles of those who watched and listened told him that. It stung him to be so easily rebuffed, and his laugh boded ugly things.

"Don't have anything to do with him," cautioned Jed as they threw their saddles under a shed. "His name's Rhues, an' he's a nasty, snaky cuss. He'll make trouble every chance he gets. Don't give him a chance!"

They went in to eat with the ranch hands. A dozen men sat at one long table and bolted immense quantities of food.

The boiled beef, the thick, lumpy gravy, the

discolored potatoes, the coarse biscuit were as strange to Danny as was his environment. His initiation back at Colt had not brought him close to such crudity as this. He tasted gingerly, and then condemned himself for being surprised to find the food good.

"You're a fool!" he told himself. "This is the real thing; you've been dabbling in unrealities so long that you've lost sense of the virtue of fundamentals. No frills here, but there's substance!"

He looked up and down at the low-bent faces, and a new joy came to him. He was out among men! Crude, genuine, real men! It was an experience, new and refreshing.

But in the midst of his contemplation it was as though fevered fingers clutched his throat. He dropped his fork, lifted the heavy cup, and drank the coffee it contained in scorching gulps.

Once more his big problem had pulled him back, and he wrestled with it—alone among men!

After the gorging the men pushed back their chairs and yawned. A desultory conversation waxed to lively banter. A match flared, and the talk came through fumes of tobacco smoke.

"Anybody got th' makin's?" asked Jed.

"Here," muttered Danny beside him, and thrust pouch and papers into his hand.

Danny followed Jed in the cigarette rolling, and they lighted from the same match with an interchange of smiles that added another strand to the bond between them.

"That's good tobacco," Jed pronounced, blowing out a whiff of smoke.

"Ought to be; it cost two dollars a pound."

Jed laughed queerly.

"Yes, it ought to," he agreed, "but we've got a tobacco out here they call Satin. Ten cents a can. *It* tastes mighty good to us."

Danny sensed a gentle rebuke, but he somehow knew that it was given in all kindliness, that it was given for his own good.

"While I fight up one way," he thought, "I must fight down another." And then aloud: "We'll stock up with your tobacco. What's liked by one ought to be good enough for —" He let the sentence trail off.

Jed answered with: "Both."

And the spirit behind that word added more strength to their uniting tie.

The day had been a hard one. Darkness came quickly, and the workers straggled off toward the bunk house. Tossing away the butt of his cigarette, Jed proposed that they turn in.

"I'm tired, and you've got a right to be," he declared.

They walked out into the cool of evening. A light flared in the bunk house, and the sound of voices raised high came to them.

"Like to look in?" Avery asked, and Danny thought he would.

Men were in all stages of undress. Some were already in their beds; others, in scant attire, stood in mid-floor and talked loudly. From one to another passed Rhues. In his hand he held a bottle, and to the lips of each man in turn he placed the neck. He faced Jed and Danny as they entered. At sight of the stranger a quick hush fell. Rhues stood there, bottle in hand, leering again.

"Jed, you don't drink," he said in his drawling, insinuating voice, "but mebby yer friend here 'uld like a nightcap."

He advanced to Danny, bottle extended, an evil smile on his face. Jed raised a hand as though to interfere; then dropped it. His jaw settled in grim resolution, his nostrils dilated, and his eyes fixed themselves fast on Danny's face.

Oh, the wailing eagerness of those abused nerves! The cracking of that tortured throat! All the weariness of the day, of the week; all the sagging of spirit under the assault of the demon in him were concentrated now. A hot wave swept his body. The fumes set the blood rushing to his eyes, to his ears; made him reel. His hand wavered up, half daring to reach for the bottle, and the strain of his drawn face dissolved in a weak smile.

Why hold off? Why battle longer? Why delay? Why? Why? Why?

Of a sudden his ears rang with memory of his father's brittle voice in cold denunciation, and the quick passing of that illusion left another talking there, in nasal twang, carrying a great sympathy.

"No, thanks," he said just above a whisper. "I'm not drinking."

He turned quickly and stepped out the door.

Through the confusion of sounds and ideas he heard the rasping laughter of Rhues, and the tone of it, the nasty, jeering note, did much to clear his brain and bring him back to the fighting.

Jed walked beside him and they crossed to where their rolls of bedding had been dropped, speaking no word. As they stooped to pick up the stuff the older man's hand fell on the boy's shoulder. His fingers squeezed, and then the palm smote Danny between the shoulder blades, soundly, confidently. Oh, that assurance! This man understood. And he had faith in this wreck of a youth that he had seen for the first time ten hours before!

Shaken, tormented though he was, weakened by the sharp struggle of a moment ago, Danny felt keenly and with something like pride that it had been worth the candle. He knew, too, with a feeling of comfort, that an explanation to Jed would never be necessary.

Silently they spread the blankets and, with a simple "Good night," crawled in between.

Danny had never before slept with his clothes on — when sober. He had never snuggled between coarse blankets in the open. But somehow it did not seem strange; it was all natural, as though it should be so.

His mind went round and round, fighting away the tingling odor that still clung in his nostrils, trying to blot out the wondering looks on the countenances of those others as they watched his struggle to refuse the stuff his tormentor held out to him.

He did not care about forgetting how Rhues's laughter sounded. Somehow the feeling of loathing for the man for a time distracted his thought from the pleading of his throat, augmented the singing of that chord his father had set in motion, bolstered his will to do, to conquer this thing!

But the effect was not enduring. On and on through the narrow channels that the fevered condition made went his thinking; forever and forever it must be so — the fighting, fighting, fighting; the searching for petty distractions that would make him forget for the moment!

Suddenly he saw that there were stars — millions upon countless millions of them dusted across the dome of the pale heavens as carelessly as a baker might dust silvered sugar over the icing of a festal cake. Big stars and tiny stars and mere little diffusive glows of light that might come from a thousand worlds, clustering together out there in infinite void. Blue stars and white stars, orange stars, and stars that glowed red. Stars that sent beams through incalculable space and stars that swung low, that seemed almost attainable. Stars that blinked sleepily and stars that stared without wavering, purposeful, attentive. Stars alone and lonely; stars in bunches. Stars in rows and patterns, as though put there with design.

Danny breathed deeply, as though the pure air were stuffy and he needed more of it, for the vagary of his wandering mind had carried him back to the place where light points were arranged by plan. He saw again the electric-light kitten and the spool of thread, the mineral-water clock, the cigarette sign with flowing border, the —

Whisky again! He moved his throbbing head from side to side.

"Is it a blank wall?" he asked quite calmly. "Shall I always come up against it? Is there no way out?"

CHAPTER V

JED PHILOSOPHIZES

MORNING: a flickering in the east that gives again to the black hold of night. Another attempt, a longer glimmer. It recedes, returns stronger; struggles, bursts from the pall of darkness, and blots out the stars before it. And after that first silver white come soft colors — shoots of violet, a wave of pink, then the golden glory of a new day.

Jed Avery yawned loud and lingeringly, pushing the blankets away from his chin with blind, fumbling motions. He thrust both arms from the covers and reached above his head, up and up and — up! until he ended with a satisfied groan. He sat erect, opening and shutting his mouth, rubbed his eyes — and stopped a motion half completed.

Danny Lenox slept with lips parted. His brown hair — the hair that wanted to curl so badly — was well down over the brow, and the skin beneath those locks was damp. One hand rested on the tarpaulin covering of the bed, the fingers in continual motion.

"Poor kid!" Jed muttered under his breath. "Poor son of a gun! He's in a jack-pot, all right, an' it'll take all any man ever had to pull —

" 'Mornin', sonny!" he cried as Danny opened his eyes and raised his head with a start.

For a moment the boy stared at him, evidencing no recognition. Then he smiled and sat up.

"How are you, Mr. Avery?"

"Well," the other began grimly, looking straight before him, "Mr. Avery's in a bad way. He died about thirty year ago."

Danny looked at him with a grin.

"But Old Jed — Old VB," he went on, "he's alive an' happy. Fancy wrappin's is for boxes of candy an' playin' cards," he explained. "They ain't necessary to men."

"I see — all right, Jed!"

Danny stared about him at the freshness of the young day.

"Wouldn't it be slick," Jed wanted to know, "if we was all fixed like th' feller who makes th' days? If yesterday's was a bad job he can start right in on this one an' make it a winner! Now, if this day turns out bad he can forget it an' begin to-morrow at sun-up to try th' job all over again!"

"Yes, it would be fine to have more chances," agreed Danny.

Jed sat silent a moment.

"Mebby so, an' mebby no," he finally recanted. "It would be slick an' easy, all right; but mebby we'd get shiftless. Mebby we'd keep puttin' off tryin' hard until next time. As 't is, we have to make every chance our only one, an' work ourselves to th' limit. Never let a chance get away! Throw it an' tie it an' hang on!"

"In other words, think it's now or never?"

Jed reached for a boot and declared solemnly: "It's th' only thing that keeps us onery human bein's on our feet an' movin' along!"

Breakfast was a brief affair, brief but enthusiastic. The gastronomic feats performed at that table were things at which to marvel, and Danny divided his thoughts between wonder at them and recalling the events of the night before. Only once did he catch Rhues's eyes, and then the leer which came from them whipped a flush high in his cheeks.

Jed and Danny rode out into the morning side by side, smoking some of the boy's tobacco. As the sun mounted and the breeze did not rise, the heat became too intense for a coat, and Danny stripped his off and tied it behind the saddle. Jed looked at the pink silk shirt a long time.

"To be sure an' that's a fine piece of goods," he finally declared.

Danny glanced down at the gorgeous garment with a mingled feeling of amusement and guilt. But he merely said:

"I thought so, too, when I bought it."

And even that little tendency toward foppishness which has been handed down to men from those ancestors who paraded in their finest skins and paints before the home of stalwart cave women seemed to draw the two closer to each other.

As though he could sense the young chap's bewilderment and wonder at the life about him, Jed related much that pertained to his own work.

"Yes, I raise some horses," he concluded, "but I sell a lot of wild ones, too. It's fun chasin' 'em, and it gets to be a habit with a feller. I like it an' can make a livin' at it, so why should I go into cattle? Those horses are out there in th' hills, runnin' wild, like some folks, an' doin' nobody no good. I catch 'em an' halter-break 'em an' they go to th' river an' get to be of use to somebody."

"Is n't it a job to catch them?" Danny asked.

"Well, I guess so!" Jed's eyes sparkled.

"Some of 'em are wiser than a bad man. Why, up in our country's a stallion that ain't never had a rope on him. Th' Captain we've got to call him. He's th' wildest an' wisest critter, horse or human, you ever see. Eight years old, an' all his life he's been chased an' never touched. He's big — not so big in weight; big like this here man Napoleon, I mean. He rules th' range. He has th' best mares on th' mountain in his bunch, an' he handles 'em like a king. We've tossed down our whole hand time an' again, but he always beats us out. We're no nearer catchin' him to-day than we was when he run a yearlin'."

The little man's voice rose shrilly and his eyes flashed until Danny, gazing on him, caught some of his fever and felt it run to the ends of his body.

"Oh, but that's a horse!" Jed went on. "Why, just to see him standin' up on the sky line, head up, tail arched-like, ready to run, not scared, just darin' us to come get him — well, it's worth a hard ride. There's somethin' about th' Captain that keeps us from hatin' him. By all natural rights somebody ought to shoot a stallion that'll run wild so long an' drive off bunches of gentle mares an' make 'em crazy wild. But no. Nobody on Red Mountain or nobody who ever chased th' Captain has wanted to harm him; yet I've heard men swear until it would make your hair curl when they was runnin' him! He's that kind. He gets to somethin' that's in real men that makes 'em light headed. I guess it's his strength. He's bigger'n tricks, that horse. He's learned all about traps an' such, an' th' way men generally catch wild horses don't bother him at all. Lordy, boy, but th' Captain's somethin' to set up nights an' talk about!"

His voice dropped on that declaration, almost in reverence.

"Well, he's so wise and strong that he'll just keep right on running free; is that the idea?" asked Danny.

Jed gnawed off a fresh chew and repocketed the plug, shifted in his saddle, and shook his head.

"Nope, I guess not," he said gravely. "I don't reckon so, because it ain't natural; it ain't th' way things is done in this world. Did you ever stop to think that of all th' strong things us men has knowed about somethin' has always turned up to be a little bit stronger? We've been all th' time pattin' ourselves on th' back an' sayin', 'There, we've gone an' done it; that'll last forever!' an' then watchin' a wind or a rain carry off what we've thought was so strong. Either that, I say, or else we've been fallin' down on our knees an' prayin' for help to stop somethin' new an' powerful that's showed up. An' when prayin' did n't do no good up pops somebody with an idea that th' Lord wants us folks to carry th' heavy end of th' load in such matters, an' gets busy workin'. An' his job ends up by makin' somethin' so strong that it satisfied all them prayers — folks bein' that unparticular that they don't mind where th' answer comes from so long as it comes an' they gets th' benefits!

"That's th' way it is all th' time. We wake up in th' mornin' an' see somethin' so discouragin' that we want to crawl back to bed an' quit tryin'; then we stop to think that nothin' has ever been so great or so strong that it kept right on havin' its own way all th' time; an' we get our sand up an' pitch in, an' pretty soon we're on top!

"All we need is th' sand to tackle big jobs; just bein' sure that they's some way of doin' or preventin' an' makin' a reg'lar hunt for that one thing. So 't is with th' Captain. He's fooled us a long time now, but some day a man'll come along who's wiser than th' Captain, an' he'll get caught.

"Nothin' strange about it. Just th' workin' out of things. 'Course, it'll all depend on th' man. Mebby some of us on th' mountain has th' brains; mebby some others has th' sand, but th' combination ain't been struck yet. We ain't *men* enough. Th' feller who catches that horse has got to be all man, just like th' feller who beats out anythin' else that's hard; got to be man all th' way through. If he's only part man an' tackles th' job he's likely to get tromped on; if he's all man, he'll do th' ridin'."

Jed stopped talking and gazed dreamily at the far horizon; dreamily, but with an eye which moved a trifle now and then to take into its range the young chap who rode beside him. Danny's head was down, facing the dust which rose from the feet of the horses ahead. The biting particles irritated the membrane of his throat, but for the moment he did not heed. "Am I a man — all the way through?" he kept asking himself. "All the way through?"

And then his nerves stung him viciously, shrieking for the stimulant which had fed them so long and so well. His aching muscles pleaded for it; his heart, miserable and lonely, missed the close, reckless friendships of those days so shortly removed, in spite of his realization of what those relations had meant; he yearned for the warming, heedless thrills; his eyes ached and called out for just the one draft that would make them alert, less hurtful.

From every joint in his body came the begging! But that chord down in his heart still vibrated; his father's arraignment was in his ears, its truth ringing clearly. The incentive to forge ahead, to stop the wasting, grew bigger, and his will stood stanch in spite of the fact that his spinning brain played such tricks as making the click of pebbles sound like the clink of ice in glasses!

Then, too, there was Jed, the big-hearted, beside him. And Jed was saying, after a long silence, as though he still thought of his theme: "Yes, sir, us men can do any old thing if we only think so! Nothin' has ever been too much for us; nothin' ever will — if we only keep on thinkin' as men ought to think an' respectin' ourselves."

Thus they traveled, side by side, the one fighting, the other uttering his homely truths and watching, always watching, noting effects, detecting temptations when the strain across the worried brow and about the tight mouth approached the breaking point. With keen intuition he went down into the young fellow and found the vibrating chord, the one that had been set humming by scorn and distrust. But instead of abusing it, instead of goading it on, Jed nursed it, fed it, strengthening the chord itself with his philosophy and his optimism.

They went on down Ant Creek, past the ranches which spread across the narrow valley. Again they slept under the open skies, and Danny once more marveled at the stars.

That second morning was agony, but Jed knew no relenting.

"You're sore an' stiff," he said, "but keepin' at a thing when it hurts is what counts, is what gets a feller well — an' that applies to more things than saddle sores, too."

He said the last as though aside, but the point carried.

At the mouth of the creek, where it flows into Clear River, they swung to the west and went downstream. Danny's condition became only semi-conscious. His head hung, his eyes were but half opened. Living resolved itself into three things. First and second: the thundering demands and the stubborn resistance of his will. When Jed spoke and roused him the remaining element come to the fore: his physical suffering. That agony became more and more acute as the miles passed, but in spite of its sharpness it required the influence of his companion's voice to awaken him to its reality.

Always, in a little back chamber of his mind, was a bit of glowing warmth — his newly born love for the man who rode beside him.

It was night when they reached the ranch.

"We're arrived, sonny! This is home!" cried Jed, slapping Danny on the shoulder. "Our home."

The boy mastered his senses with an effort.

When he dismounted he slumped to one knee and Jed had to help him stand erect.

Danny remembered nothing of the bed going, nor could he tell how long the little, gray-haired man stood over him, muttering now and then, rubbing his palms together; nor of how, when he turned toward the candle on the table, burning steadily and brightly there in the night like a young Crusader fighting back the shadows into the veriest corner of the room, his eyes were misted.

It was a strange awakening, that which followed. Danny felt as though he had slept through a whole phase of his existence. At first he was not conscious of his surroundings, did not try to remember where he was or what had gone before. He lay on his back, mantled in a strange peace, wonderfully content. Torture seemed to have left him, bodily torments had fled. His heart pumped slowly; a vague, pleasing weakness was in his bones. It was rest — rest after achievement, the achievement of stability, the arrival at a goal.

Then, breaking into full consciousness, his nostrils detected odors. He sniffed slightly, scarcely knowing that he did so. Cooking! It was unlike other smells from places of cookery that he had known; it was attractive, compelling.

All that had happened since his departure from Colt came back to him with his first movement. His body was a center of misery, as though it were shot full of needles, as though it had been stretched on a rack, then blistered.

Dressing was accomplished to the accompaniment of many grunts and quick intakings of breath.

When he tried to walk he found that the process was necessarily slow—slower than it had ever been before. Setting each foot before the other gingerly, as if in experiment, he walked across the tiny room toward the larger apartment of the cabin.

"Mornin'!" cried Jed, closing the oven door with a gentleness that required the service of both hands. "I allowed you'd be up about now. Just step outside an' wash an' it'll be about ready. Can you eat? Old VB sure can build a breakfast, an' he's never done better than this."

"By the smell, I judge so," said Danny.

The warm breath of baking biscuits came to him from the oven. A sputtering gurgle on the stove told that something fried. The aroma of coffee was in the air, too, and Jed lifted eggs from a battered pail to drop them into a steaming kettle. The table, its plain top scrubbed to whiteness, was set for two, and the sunlight that streamed through the window seemed to be all caught and concentrated in a great glass jar of honey that served as a centerpiece.

Danny's eyes and nostrils and ears took it all in as he moved toward the outer doorway. When he gained it he paused, a hand on the low lintel, and looked out upon his world.

Away to the south stretched the gulch, rolling of bottom, covered with the gray-green sage. Over east rose the stern wall, scarred and split, with cedars clinging in the interstices, their forms dark green against the saffron of the rocks. Up above, towering into the unstained sky of morning, a rounded, fluted peak, like the crowning achievement of some vast cathedral.

The sun was just in sight above the cliff, but Danny knew that day was aging, and felt, with his peace, a sudden sharp affection for the old man who, with an indulgence that was close to motherly, had let him sleep. It made him feel young and incompetent, yet it was good, comforting — like the peace of that great stillness about him.

Except for the soft sounds from the stove, there was no break. Above, on the ridges, a breeze might be blowing; but not an intimation of it down here. Just quiet — silvery and holy.

The sun shoved itself clear of the screening trees. A jack rabbit, startled by nothing at all, sprang from its crouching under a brush shelter and made off across the gulch with the jerky lightness of a stone skipping on water. As he bobbed the grass and bushes dewdrops flew from them, catching sunbeams as they hurtled out to their death, for one instant of wondrous glory flashing like gems.

Danny Lenox, late of New York, drew a deep, quivering breath and leaned his head against the crude doorway. He was sore and weak and felt almost hysterical, but perhaps this was only because he was so happy!

CHAPTER VI

AMBITION IS BORN

AND then began Danny's apprenticeship. Jed, the wise, did not delay activity. He commenced with the boy as soon as breakfast had been eaten and the dishes washed.

That first day they shod a horse, Danny doing nothing really, but taking orders from Jed as though the weight of a vast undertaking rested on his shoulders.

The next day they mended fences from early morning until evening.

Gradually the realization came to Danny that he was doing something, that he was filling a legitimate place — small, surely: nevertheless he was being of use, he was creating. A pleasing sensation! One of the few truly wholesome delights he had ever experienced. Danny thought about it with almost childish happiness; then, letting his mind return again to the established rut, he was surprised to know that mere thinking about his simple, homely duties had stilled for the time it endured the restless creature within him.

The boy's bodily hurts righted themselves. Long hours of sleep did more than anything else to speed recovery. Those first two nights he

AMBITION IS BORN

was between covers before darkness came to the gulch, and Jed let him sleep until the sun was well up.

On the third evening they sat outside, Danny watching Jed put a new half-sole on a cast-off riding boot.

"They're your size," the old man said, "an' you'll have to wear boots, to be sure. Them things you got on ain't what I'd call exactly fitted to ridin' a horse."

Danny looked down at his modish Oxfords and smiled. Then he glanced up at the man beside him, who hammered and cut and grunted while he worked as though his very immortality depended on getting those boots ready for his new hand to wear.

Oh, the boy from the city could not then appreciate the big feeling of man for mankind which prompted such humble labor. It was a labor of love, the mere mending of that stiff old boot! In it Jed Avery found the encompassing happiness which comes to those who understand, happiness of the same sort he had felt back there at Colt when he saw that there was a human being who needed help and that it was in his power to give him that help. And the peace this happiness engendered created an atmosphere which soothed and made warm the heart of the boy, though he did not know why.

"Guess we'd better move inside an' get a light," Jed muttered finally. "I'll shut the corral gate. You light th' candle, will you? It's on th' shelf over th' table — stickin' in a bottle."

Danny watched him go away into the dusk and heard the creak of the big gate swinging shut before he stepped into the house and groped his way along for the shelf. He found it after a moment and fumbled along for the candle Jed had said was there. His fingers closed on something hard and cold and cylindrical. He slid his fingers upward; then staggered back with a half-cry.

"What's wrong?" asked Jed, coming into the house.

Danny did not answer him, so the old man stepped forward toward the shelf. In a moment a match flared; the cold wick of the candle took the flame, warmed, sent it higher, and a glow filled the room.

The boy looked out from eyes that were dark and wide and filled with the old horror. The hand held near his lips shook, and he turned on Jed a look that pleaded, then gazed back at the light.

The candle was stuck in the neck of a whisky bottle.

Danny opened his lips to speak, but the words would not come. That terror was back again, shattering his sense of peace, melting the words in his throat with its heat.

Jed moved near to him.

"It's a bright light — for such a little candle," he said slowly, and a stout assurance was in his tone.

"But I — I touched the bottle — in the dark!'

Danny's voice was high and strained, and the words, when finally they did come, tripped over one another in nervous haste. His knees were weak under him. Such was the strength of the tentacles which reached up to stay his struggles and to drag him back into the depths from which he willed to rise. Such was the weakness of the nervous system on which the strain of the ordeal was placed.

Jed put a hand on the boy's shoulder and gazed into the drawn face.

"It's all right, sonny," he said softly, his voice modulating from twang to tenderness in the manner it had. "Most men touches it in th' dark. But don't you see what this bottle's for? Don't you see that candle? Burnin' away there, corkin' up th' bottle, givin' us light so we can see?"

Then the other hand went up to the boy's other shoulder, and the little old rancher shook young Danny Lenox gently, as though to joggle him back to himself.

"I know, sonny," he said softly. "I know —" Then he turned away quickly and smote his palms together with a sharp crack.

"Now get to bed. I'll finish these here boots to-night and in th' mornin' we ride. If you're goin' to get to be a top hand, we've got to quit foolin' around home an' get to learn th' country. They's a lot of colts we got to brand an' a bunch of wild ones to gather. It means work — lots of it — for you an' me!"

He set to work, busily thumping on the boot.

In the morning, Danny was subdued, subdued and shaking. The spontaneity that had characterized his first days on the ranch had departed. He was still eager for activity, but not for the sake of the new experiences in themselves. That gnawing was again in his throat, tearing his flesh, it seemed, and to still the trembling of his hand it was necessary for him to clutch the saddle horn and keep his fingers clamped tightly about it as they rode along.

They climbed out of the gulch, horses picking their way up an almost impossible trail, and on a high ridge, where country rolled and tossed about them for immeasurable distances, Jed stopped and pointed out the directions to his companion.

Thirty miles to the south was Clear River with its string of ranches, and the town of Ranger, their post office. Twenty miles to the southeast was the S Bar S Ranch, the center of the country's cattle activity, and over west, on Sand Creek, a dozen miles' ride across the hills and double that distance by road, was another scattering of ranches where Dick Worth, deputy sheriff for that end of Clear River County, lived.

"An' to th' north of us," continued Jed, with a sweep of his hand, "they's nothin' but hills — clean to Wyoming! We're on th' outskirts of settlements. South of th' river it's all ranches, but north — nothin'. Couple of summer camps but no ranches. It's a great get-away country, all right!"

The riding was easy that day, and in spite of his stiffness Danny wished it were harder, because the turmoil kept up within him, and even the unbroken talk of Jed, giving him an intelligent, interesting idea of the country, could not crowd out his disquieting thoughts.

But it was easier the next day, and Danny took a deep interest in the hunt for a band of mares with colts that should be branded. Jed's low, warning "H-s-s-t! There they are!" set his heart pounding wildly, and he listened eagerly to the directions the old man gave him; then he waited in high excitement while Jed circled and got behind the bunch.

The horses came toward him, and Danny, at Jed's shout, commenced to ride for the ranch. It was a new, an odd, an interesting game. The horses came fast and faster. Now and then to his ears floated Jed's repeated cry: "Keep goin'! Keep ahead!" And he spurred on, wondering at every jump how his horse could possibly keep his feet longer in that awful footing.

But he had faith in the stout little beast he rode, and his spirit was of the sort that would not question when a man as skilled in the game as was Jed urged him along.

The mares with their colts pressed closely, but Danny kept going, kept urging speed. Straight on for the ranch he headed, and when they reached the level bottom of the gulch the race waxed warm.

"Into th' round corral!" cried Jed. "Keep goin'! You're doin' fine!"

And into the round corral Danny headed his mount, while the nose of the lead mare reached out at his pony's flank.

The gate swung shut; the mares trotted around the inclosure, worried, for there their offspring had been taken from them before. The colts hung close to their mothers, snorting and rolling their wide eyes, while the saddle horses stood with legs apart, getting their wind.

Danny's eyes sparkled.

"That's sport!" he declared. "But, say, will these horses always follow a rider that way?"

Jed loosed his cinch before he answered: "Horses is like some men. As long as they're bein' pushed from behind an' they's somebody goin' ahead of 'em, they'll follow — follow right through high water! But once let 'em get past th' rider who's supposed to be holdin' 'em up — why, then they's no handlin' 'em at all. They scatter an' go their own way, remainin' free.

"As I said, they're like men. To be sure, lots of men has got to give that what's leadin' 'em such a run that they beat it to death an' get a chance to go free!"

Danny rubbed his horse's drenched withers and agreed with a nod as Jed walked over to the gate and fumbled with the fastening.

"Say," he said, turning round, "I like th' way you ride!"

Danny looked up quickly, pleased.

"I'm glad," he said, but in the simple assertion was a great self-pride.

"Most fellers strange in th' country would n't fancy takin' that kind of a bust down off a point. No, sir. Not such a ride for us old heads, but for a greenhorn — Well, I guess you 'll get to be a top hand some day, all right!"

And the influence which more than all else was to help Danny become a top hand, which was to set up in his heart the great ambition, which was to hold itself up as a blazing ideal, came early in his novitiate as a horse hunter — came in a fitting setting, on a day richly golden, when the air seemed filled with a haze of holy incense, holy with the holiness of beauty. It was one of those mountain days when the immensity of nature becomes so obvious and so potent that even the beasts leave off their hunting or their grazing to gaze into wondrous distances. The sage is green and brash in the near sunlight, soft and purple out yonder; the hills sharp and hard and detailed under the faultless sky for unthinkable miles about, then soft and vague, melting in color and line, rolling, reaching, tossing in a repetition of ranges until eyes ache in following them and men are weak about their middles from the feeling of vastnesses to which measurements by figures are profane.

Jed and Danny searched for horses along two parallel ridges. Now and then they saw each other, but for the most part it had been a day of solitary riding.

Late afternoon arrived, and Danny had about abandoned hope of success. He was considering the advisability of mounting the ridge above the gulch into which he had ridden and locating Jed, though loath to leave the solitudes.

His pony picked them out and stopped before Danny's eyes registered the sight. The boy searched quickly, and over against a clump of cedars, halfway up the rise, he saw horses.

"No, that's not they," he muttered. "Jed said there were two white mares among them. Not—"

His pony started under him, gave a sharp little shudder, then moved a step backward and stood still, a barely perceptible tremor shaking his limbs.

Then a sound new and strange came to Danny. He did not know its origin, but it contained a quality that sent a thrill pulsing from his heart. Shrill it was, but not sharply cut, wavering but not breaking; alarm, warning, concern, caution — the whistle of a stallion! Then silence, while the mares stood rigid and the saddle horse held his breath.

Again it came, and a quick chill struck down Danny's spine. His searching eyes encountered the source. There, halfway between the mares and the crown of the ridge he stood, out on a little rim-rock that made a fitting pedestal, alert, defiant, feet firmly planted, with the poise of a proud monarch.

Even across the distance his coat showed the glossiness seen only on fine, short hair; his chest, turned halfway toward the rider, was splendid in breadth and depth, indicating superb strength, endurance, high courage. Danny looked with a surge of appreciation at the arch of the neck, regal in its slim strength, at the fine, straight limbs, clean as a dancing girl's; at the long, lithe barrel with its fine symmetry.

A wandering breath of breeze came up the gulch, fluttering the wealth of tail, lifting the heavy mane and forelock. The horse raised a front foot and smote the ledge on which he stood as though wrath rose that a mere man should ride into his presence, and he would demand departure or homage from Danny Lenox. He shook his noble head impatiently, to clear his eyes of the hair that blew about them. And once more came the whistle.

The mares stirred. One, a bright buckskin, trotted up the rise a dozen yards, and stopped to turn and look. The others moved slowly, eyes and ears for Danny.

Again the whistle; a clatter of loosened stones

as the black leader bounded up the hillside; and the bunch was away in his wake.

"The Captain!" Danny breathed, and then, in a cry which echoed down the gulch — "The Captain!"

He was scarcely conscious of his movements, but his quirt fell, his spurs raked the sides of his pony, and the sturdy little animal, young and not yet fully developed, doing his best in making up the ridge, labored effectively, perhaps drawn on by that same raw desire which went straight to the roots of Danny's spirit and came back to set the fires glowing in his eyes.

The boy rode far forward in his saddle, his gaze on the plunging band that scattered stones and dirt as they strove for the top. But he was many lengths behind when the last mare disappeared over the rim. He fanned his pony again, and the beast grunted in his struggles for increased speed in the climbing, lunging forward with mighty efforts which netted so little ground.

As he toiled up the last yards Danny saw the Captain again, standing there against the sky, watching, waiting, mane and tail blowing about him. His strong, full, ever delicate body quivered with the singing spirit of confidence within him and communicated itself to the weakling pursuer. Just a glimpse of the man was all that the black horse wanted, then — he was off.

As Danny's horse caught the first stride in the run down the ridge he saw the Captain stretch that fine nose out to the flank of a lagging mare, and saw the animal throw her head about in pain as the strong teeth nipped her flesh, commanding more speed.

Danny Lenox was mad! He pulled off his hat and beat his pony's withers with it. He cried aloud the Captain's name. He went on and on, dropping far down on his horse's side as they brushed under the cedars, settling firmly to the seat when the animal leaped over rocks. His shirt was open at the neck, and his throat was chilled with the swift rush of air, while hot blood swirled close to the skin. His eyes glowed with the fire set there by this new fascination, the love of beautiful strength; and through his body sang the will to conquer!

It was an unfair race. Danny and his light young horse had no chance. Off and away drew the stallion and his bunch, without effort after that first crazy break down the ridge. The last Danny saw of him was with head turned backward, nose lifted, as though he breathed disdainful defiance at the man who would come in his wake with the thirst for possession high within him!

And so the boy pulled up, dropped off, and let his breathing pony rest. His legs were uncertain under him, and he knew that his pulses raced. For many minutes he strove to analyze his emotion but could not.

Jed slid off the next ridge and came up at a trot. His face was radiant. "Well, he got you, did n't he?" He laughed aloud.

"I thought he would, all along; and I knowed he had you when I see you break up over th' ridge. You've got th' fever now, like a lot of th' rest of us! Mebby you'll chase horses here for years, but you'll always have an eye out for just one thing — th' Captain. You won't be satisfied until you've got him — like all of us; not satisfied until we've done th' biggest thing there is in sight to do."

Then, as though parenthetically: "An' when we've done that we've only h'isted ourselves up to where we can see that they's a hunderd times as much to do."

"Gad, but he goes right into a fellow's heart!" breathed Danny, looking into the sunset. "I did n't know I was following him, Jed, until the pony here commenced to tire."

He laughed apologetically, as though confessing a foolishness, but his face was glowing with a new light. A fresh incentive had come to him with this awakening admiration, inciting him to emulation. The spirit of the stallion stirred in him again that vibrant chord which had been urging him to fight on, not to give up.

His ambition to overcome his weakness began to take quick, definite direction. Added to the effort of overcoming his vices would henceforth be the endeavor to achieve, to compass some worthy object. This was his aim: to be a leader to whom men would turn for inspiration; to be unconquerable among men, as the Captain was unconquerable among his kind.

AMBITION IS BORN

As the ideal took shape, springing full-born from his excitement, Danny Lenox felt lifted above himself, felt stronger than human strength, felt as though he were forever beyond human weaknesses.

When they had ridden twenty minutes in silence Jed broke out: "Sonny, I don't want to act like 'n old woman, but I guess I'm gettin' childish! I've knowed you less than a month. I don't even know who you was when you come. We don't ask men about theirselves when they come in here. What a feller wants to tell, we take; what he keeps to hisself we wonder at without mentionin' it.

"But you, sonny — you couldn't keep it from me. I know what it is, I know. I seen it when you got off th' train at Colt — seen that somethin' had got you down. I knowed for sure what it was when you stopped by th' saloon there. I knowed how honest you was with yourself in that little meetin' with Rhues. I know all about it — 'cause I've been through th' same thing — alone, an' years ago."

After a pause he went on: "An' just now, when I seen you comin' down that ridge after th' Captain, I knowed th' right stuff was in you — because when a thing like that horse touches a man off it's a sign he's th' right kind, th' kind that wants to do things for th' sake of knowin' his own strength. You've got th' stuff in you to be a man, but you're fightin' an awful fight.

You need help; you ought to have friends — you ought to have a daddy!"

He gulped, and for a dozen strides there were no more words.

"I feel like adoptin' you, sonny, 'cause I know. I feel like makin' you a part of this here outfit, which ain't never branded a colt that did n't belong to it, which ain't never done nothin' but go straight ahead an' be honest with itself, good times an' bad.

"I used to be proud when they called me Old VB, 'cause they all knowed th' brand was on th' level, an' when they, as you might say, put it on me, I felt like I was wearin' some sort of medal. I feel just like makin' you part of th' VB — Young VB — 'cause I can help you here an' — an' 'fore God A'mighty you need help, man that you are!"

An hour and a half later, when the last dish had been wiped, when the dishpan had been hung away, Danny spoke the next words. He walked close to the old man, his face quiet under the new consciousness of how far he must go to approach this new ideal. He took the hard old hand in his own, covered its back with the other, and muttered in a voice that was far from clear: "Good night, Old VB."

And the other, to cover the tenderness in his tone, snapped back: "Get to bed, Young VB; they's that ahead of you to-morrow which'll take every bit of your courage and strength!"

CHAPTER VII

WITH HOOF AND TOOTH

SO IT came to pass that Danny Lenox of New York ceased to exist, and a new man took his place — Young VB, of Clear River County, Colorado.

"Who's your new hand?" a passing rider asked Jed one morning, watching with interest as the stranger practiced with a rope in the corral.

"Well, sir, he's th' ridin'est tenderfoot you ever see!" Jed boasted. "I picked him up out at Colt an' put him to work — after Charley went away."

"Where'd he come from? What's his name?" the other insisted.

"From all appearances, he ain't of these parts," replied Jed, squinting at a distant peak. "An' around here we've got to callin' him Young VB."

The rider, going south, told a man he met that Jed had bestowed his brand on a human of another generation. Later, he told it in Ranger. The man he met on the road told it on Sand Creek; those who heard it in Ranger bore it off into the hills, for even such a small bit of news is a meaty morsel for those who sit in the same small company about bunk-house stoves months on end.

The boy became known by name about the country, and those who met him told others what the stranger was like. Men were attracted by his simplicity, his desire to learn, by his frank impulse to be himself yet of them.

"Oh, yes, he's th' feller," they would recall, and then recite with the variations that travel gives to tales the incident that transpired in the Anchor bunk house.

Young VB fitted smoothly into the work of the ranch. He learned to ride, to rope, to shoot, to cook, and to meet the exigencies of the range; he learned the country, cultivated the instinct of directions. And, above all, he learned to love more than ever the little old man who fathered and tutored him.

And Young VB became truly useful. It was not all smooth progress. At times — and they were not infrequent — the thirst came on him with vicious force, as though it would tear his will out by the roots.

The fever which that first run after the Captain aroused, and which made him stronger than doubtings, could not endure without faltering. The ideal was ever there, but at times so elusive! Then the temptings came, and he had to fight silently, doggedly.

Some of these attacks left him shaking in spite of his mending nerves — left him white in spite of the brown that sun and wind put on him. During the daytime it was bad enough, but when he woke in the night, sleep broken sharply, and raised unsteady hands to his begging throat, there was not the assuring word from Jed, or the comfort of his companionship.

The old man took a lasting pride in Danny's adaptability. His comments were few indeed, but when the boy came in after a day of hard, rough, effective toil, having done all that a son of the hills could be expected to do, the little man whistled and sang as though the greatest good fortune in the world had come to him.

One morning Jed went to the corral to find VB snubbing up an unbroken sorrel horse they had brought in the day before. He watched from a distance, while the young man, after many trials, got a saddle on the animal's back.

"Think you can?" he asked, his eyes twinkling, as he crawled up on the aspen poles to watch.

"I don't know, Jed, but it's time I found out!" was the answer, and in it was a click of steely determination.

It was not a nice ride, not even for the short time it lasted. Young VB "went and got it" early in the mêlée. He clung desperately to the saddle horn with one hand, but with the other he plied his quirt and between every plunge his spurs raked the sides of the bucking beast.

He did not know the art of such riding, but the courage was there and when he was thrown it was only at the moment when the sorrel put into the battle his best.

VB got to his feet and wiped the dust from his eyes.

"Hurt?" asked Jed.

"Nothing but my pride," muttered the boy. He grasped the saddle again, got one foot in the stirrup, and, after being dragged around the inclosure, got to the seat.

Again he was thrown, and when he arose and made for the horse a third time Jed slipped down from the fence to intervene.

"Not again to-day," he said, with a pride that he could not suppress. "Take it easy; try him again to-morrow."

"But I don't want to give up!" protested the boy. "I *can* ride that horse."

"You ain't givin' up; I made you," the other smiled. "You ought to have been born in the hills. You'd have made a fine bronc twister. Ain't it a shame th' way men are wasted just by bein' born out of place?"

VB seemed not to hear. He rubbed the nose of the frantic horse a moment, then said:

"If I could get this near the Captain — Jed, if I could ever get a leg over that stallion he'd be mine or I'd die trying!"

"Still thinkin' of him?"

"All the time! I never forget him. That fellow has got into my blood. He's the biggest thing in this country — the strongest — and I want to show him that there's something a little stronger, something that can break the power he's held so long — and that *I* am that something!"

"That's considerable ambition," Jed said, casually, though he wanted to hug the boy.

"I know it. Most people out here would think me a fool if they heard me talk this way. Me, a greenhorn, a tenderfoot, talking crazily about doing what not one of you has ever been able to do!"

"Not exactly, VB. It's th' wantin' to do things bad enough that makes men do 'em, remember. This feller busted you twice, but you've got th' stuff under your belt that makes horses behave. That's th' only stuff that'll ever make th' Captain anything but th' wild thing he is now. Sand! *Grit!* Th' *wantin'* to do it!"

A cautious whistle from Jed that afternoon called VB into a thicket of low trees, from where he looked down on a scene that drove home even more forcibly the knowledge of the strength of spirit that was incased in the glossy coat of the great stallion.

"Look!" the old man said in a low voice, pointing into the gulch. "It's a Percheron — one of Thorpe's stallions. He's come into th' Captain's band an' they're goin' to fight!"

VB looked down on the huge gray horse, heavier by three hundred pounds than the black, stepping proudly along over the rough gulch bottom, tossing his head, twisting it about on his neck, his ears flat, his tail switching savagely.

Up the far rise huddled the mares. The Captain was driving the last of them into the bunch as VB came in sight. That done, he turned to watch the coming of the gray.

Through the stillness the low, malicious, muffled crying of the Percheron came to them clearly as he pranced slowly along, parading his graces for the mares up there, displaying his strength to their master, who must come down and battle for his sovereignty.

The Captain stood and watched as though mildly curious, standing close to his mares. His tail moved slowly, easily, from side to side. His ears, which had been stiffly set forward at first, slowly dropped back.

The gray drew nearer, to within fifty yards, forty, thirty. He paused, pawed the ground, and sent a great puff of dust out behind him.

Then he swung to the left and struck up the incline, headed directly for the Captain, striding forward to humble him under the very noses of his mares — the band that would be the prize of that coming conflict!

He stopped again and pawed spitefully. He rose on his hind legs slowly, head shaking, forefeet waving in the air, as though flexing his muscles before putting them to the strain of combat.

He settled to the ground barely in time, for with a scream of rage the black horse hurtled.

He seemed to be under full speed at the first leap, and the speed was terrific!

Foam had gathered on his lips, and the rush down the pitch flung it spattering against his glossy chest. His shrilling did not cease from the time he left his tracks until, with front hoofs raised, a catapult of living, quivering hate, he hurled himself at the gray. It ended then in a wail of frenzy — not of fear, but of royal rage at the thought of any creature offering challenge!

The gray dropped back to all fours, whirled sharply, and took the impact at a glancing blow, a hip cringing low as the ragged hoofs of the black crashed upon it. The Captain stuck his feet stiffly into the ground, plowing great ruts in the earth in his efforts to stop and turn and meet the rush of the other, as he recovered from the first shock, gathered headway, and bore down on him. He overcame his momentum, turning as he came to a stop, lifted his voice again, and rose high to meet hoof for hoof the ponderous attack that the bigger animal turned on him.

The men above heard the crash of their meeting. The impact of flesh against flesh was terrific. For the catch of an instant the horses seemed to poise, the Captain holding against the fury that had come upon him, holding even against the odds of lightness and up-hill fighting. Then they swayed to one side, and VB uttered a low cry of joy as the Captain's teeth buried themselves in the back of the Percheron's neck.

Close together then they fought, throwing dirt and stones, ripping up the brush as their rumbling feet found fresh hold and then tore away the earth under the might that was brought to bear in the assault and resistance. A dozen times they rushed upon each other, a dozen times they parted and raised for fresh attack. And each time the gray body and the black met in smacking crash it was the former that gave way, notwithstanding his superior weight.

"Look at him!" whispered Jed. "Look at that cuss! He hates that gray so that he's got th' fear of death in him! Look at them ears! Hear him holler! He's too quick. Too quick, an' he's got th' spirit that makes up th' difference in weight — an' more, too!"

He stopped with a gasp as the Captain, catching the other off balance, smote him on the ribs with his hoofs until the blows sounded like the rumble of a drum. The challenger threw up his head in agony and cringed beneath the torment, running sidewise with bungling feet.

"He like to broke his back!" cried Jed.

"And look at him bite!" whispered VB.

The Captain tore at the shoulders and neck of the gray horse with his gleaming, malevolent teeth. Again and again they found fleshhold, and his neck bowed with the strength he put into the wrenching, while his feet kept up their terrific hammering.

No pride of challenge in the gray now; no

display of graces for the onlooking mares; no attacking; just impotent resistance, as the Captain drove him on and on down the gulch, humbled, terrified, routed.

The sounds of conflict became fainter as the Percheron strove to make his escape and the Captain relentlessly followed him, the desire to kill crying from his every line.

The battling beasts rounded a point of rocks, and the two men sprang to their horses to follow the moving fight. But they were no more than mounted when the Captain came back, swinging along in his wonderful trot, ears still flat, head still shaking, anger possessing him — anger and pride.

He was unmarked by the conflict, save with sweat and dust and foam; he was still possessed of his superb strength. He went up the pitch to his band with all the vigor of stride he had displayed in flying from it to answer the presumption of the gray. And the mares, watching him, seemed to draw long breaths, dropped their heads to the bunch grass, and, one by one, moved along in their grazing.

Jed looked at VB. What he saw in the boy's face made him nod his head slowly in affirmation.

"You're that sort, too," he whispered exultingly. "You're that sort! *His* kind!"

CHAPTER VIII

A Head of Yellow Hair

THE next day Jed declared for a trip to Ranger after grub. The trip was necessary, and it would be an education for VB, he said with a chuckle, to see the town. But when they were ready to start a rider approached the ranch.

"If it ain't Kelly!" Jed cried. Then, in explanation: "He's a horse buyer, an' must be comin' to see me."

And the man's desire to look over the VB stuff was so strong that Jed declared it would be business for him to stay at home.

In a way, Danny was glad of the opportunity to go alone. It fed the glowing pride in his ability to do things, to be of use, and after a short interchange of drolleries with the man Kelly, whom he instinctively liked, the boy mounted to the high wagon seat and drove off down the gulch.

It was a long drive, and hours alone are conducive to thought. Danny's mind went back over the days that had passed, wandering along those paths he had followed since that July morning in the luxuriously dim house on Riverside Drive. And the reason for his departing from the old way came back to him now, because he was alone, with nothing to divert his attention. The old turbulence arose; it wore and wore with the miles, eating down to his will, teasing, coaxing, threatening, pleading, fuming.

"Will it always be so?" he asked the distances. "When it comes to challenge me, to take away all that I hold dear, shall I always be afraid? Shan't I be able to stand and fight and triumph, merely raging because it dares tempt me instead of fearing this thing itself?"

And he spoke as he thought in terms of his ideal, as materialized in the Captain.

"But will it always be so with him?" he asked again. "Won't some horse come to challenge him some day and batter him down and make defeat all the more bitter because of the supremacy he has enjoyed? Would it then be — worth the candle?"

And as he bowed his head he thought once more of the beacon in the bottle, corking it up, driving back the shadows, making a livable place in the darkness.

Nothing is ever intrinsically curious. Curiousness comes solely from relationships. Time and place are the great factors in creating oddities. Five miles farther on VB saw a curious thing. This was at the forks of the road. To his right it went off behind the long, rocky point toward Sand Creek; to the left it wandered through the sage brush over toward the S Bar S

Ranch, and ahead it ran straight on to Ranger.

Along the prong that twisted to the left went an automobile. Nothing curious about that to VB, for many times he had seen Bob Thorpe driving his car through the country.

But at the wheel was a lone figure crowned by a mass of yellow hair. That was the curious thing he saw!

All VB could distinguish at that distance with his hot eyes was yellow hair. The machine picked its way carefully along the primitive road, checking down here, shooting ahead there, going on toward the horizon, bearing the yellow hair away from him, until it was only a crawling thing with a long, floating tail of dust. But it seemed to him he could still make out that bright fleck even after the automobile had become indistinguishable.

"She's alone," muttered VB. "She's driving that car alone — and out here!"

Then he wondered with a laugh why he should think it so strange. Many times he had ridden down Fifth Avenue in the afternoon traffic congestion beside a woman who piloted her own car. Surely the few hazards of this thoroughfare were not to be compared with that!

But it was the incongruity which his association of ideas brought up that made him tingle a little. That hair! It did not belong out here. He had not been near enough to see the girl's face — he was sure it was a girl, not a grown woman — but the color of her crowning adornment suggested many and definite things. And those things were not of these waste places; were not rough and primal. They were finer, higher.

Once before he had experienced this nameless, pleasurable sensation of being familiar with the unknown. That had been when Jed had sketched with a dozen unrelated words a picture of the daughter of the house of Thorpe.

The motor car with its fair-haired pilot had been gone an hour when Danny, watching a coyote skulk among distant rocks, said aloud: "East — college — I'll bet — I — I wonder —"

Dusk had come when Young VB entered Ranger and put up at the ranch, which made as much pretense of buildings as did the town itself. Morning found him weak and drawn, as it always did after a night of the conflict, yet he was up with the sun, eager to be through with his task and back with Jed.

Purchasing supplies is something of a rite in Ranger, and under other conditions, on another day perhaps, it might have amused VB; but with the unrest within him he found little about the procedure that did not irritate.

In the store there one may buy everything in hardware from safety pins to trace chains; groceries range from canned soup to wormy nuts; in drugs anything, bounded on one end by horse liniment and on the other extreme by eye-drops guaranteed to prevent cataracts, is for sale; and overalls and sewing silk are alike popular commodities. All is in fine order, and the manager is a walking catalogue of household necessities.

VB was relieved when the buying had been accomplished. He crowded a can of ten-cent tobacco into the pocket of his new overalls and started for the team. A dozen strides away from the store building he paused to look about. It was his first inspection of Ranger in daylight, and now as he surveyed its extent his sense of humor rose above the storm within him, and he grinned.

The store, with its conventional false front, stood beside the post office, which was built as a lean-to. Next to it was a building of red corrugated iron, and sounds of blacksmithing issued from it. Behind VB was a tiny house, with a path running from it to the store, the home of the manager. Next it a log cabin. Down at the left, near the river, was another house, deserted, the ranch where he had stayed, and beyond it a trio of small shacks on the river bank.

"Ranger," he muttered, and chuckled.

The road, brown and soft with fine dust, stretched on and on toward Utah, off to the west where silence was supreme.

The buildings were all on the north side of the road.

"A south front was the idea, I suppose," VB murmured. "Mere matter of —"

His gaze had traveled across the road to a

one building erected there, far back against a sharp rise of ground. It stood apart, as though consciously aloof from the rest, a one-story structure, and across its front a huge white sign, on which in black characters was painted the word:

SALOON

Unconsciously his tongue came out to wet the parched lips and his fingers plucked at the seams of the new overalls.

Why not? the insidious self argued, why not? All changes must come gradually. Nothing can be accomplished in a moment. Just one drink to cool his throat, to steady his nerves, and brace him for the fight he would make — later.

As he stood there listening to that inner voice, yet holding it off, he did not hear the fall of hoofs behind him or the jingle of spurs as a rider dismounted and approached.

But he did hear the voice — drawling, nasty, jeering:

"Was you considerin' havin' a bit o' refreshment, stranger?"

VB wheeled quickly and looked straight into the green glitter of Rhues's red-lidded eyes. The cruel mouth was stretched in an angular grin, and the whole countenance expressed the incarnate spirit of the bully.

Into Danny's mind leaped the idea that this thing before him, this evil-eyed, jeering, leering, daring being, typified all that was foul in his heart — just as the Captain typified all that was virtuous.

The intuitive repulsion surged to militant hate. He wanted to smother the breath which kept alive such a spirit, wanted to stamp into the dust the body that housed it — because it mocked him and tempted him! But Young VB only turned and brushed past the man without a word.

He heard Rhues's laughter behind him, and heard him call: "Ranger ain't no eastern Sunday school. Better have one an' be a man, like th' rest o' th' boys!"

However, when Rhues turned back to his pony the laugh was gone and he was puzzling over something. After he had mounted, he looked after the boy again maliciously.

VB was on the road in half an hour, driving the horses as fast as he dared. He wanted to be back in Jed's cabin, away from Ranger. This thing had followed him across the country to Colt; from Colt to the Anchor; and now It lurked for him in Ranger. The ranch was his haven.

The settlement by the river reached its claws after him as he drove, fastening them in his throat and shaking his will until it seemed as though it had reached the limit of its endurance.

It was dark when he reached home. A mile away he had seen the light and smiled weakly at thought of it, and the horses, more than willing, carried the wagon over the remaining distance with a bouncing that threatened its contents.

When VB pulled up before the outer gate Jed hurried from the cabin.

"VB," he called, "are you all right?"

"All right, Jed," he answered, dropping from the seat.

And the boy thought he heard the older man thank his God.

Without words, they unharnessed and went to the cabin. Kelly was sleeping loudly in the adjoining room. The table had been moved from its usual place nearer to the window, and the bottle with its burning candle was close against the pane. Jed looked at the candle, than at VB.

"I'm sorry," he said, seeing the strain about the boy's mouth. "I never thought about it until come night, Young VB. I never thought about it. I — I guess I'm an old fool, gettin' scared th' way I do. So I shoved this candle up against th' window — because I'm an old fool and thought — it might help a little."

And VB answered: "It does help, Jed! Every little thing helps. And oh, God, how I need it!"

He turned away.

CHAPTER IX

Pursuit

SUMMER drew toward its close and the work became more exacting. Jed was sure that more of his colts ran the range without brands, and the two rode constantly, searching every gulch and break for the strays. One day they went far to the east, and at noon encountered three of Bob Thorpe's men building fence.

"It's his new drift fence," Jed explained. "He's goin' to have a lot of winter pasture, to be sure he is. It'll help us, too. When we come takin' these here willow tails off this ridge they'll find somethin' new. It's so close up to the foot of the rise that they can't jump it."

"Thorpe must be rich," remarked Young VB as they went on along the fence.

"Rich don't say it! He's rollin' in money, an' he sure knows how to enjoy it. Every winter, when things gets squared away, he takes his wife an' goes to California. I s'pose he'll be takin' his girl, too — now that she's quit goin' to school."

The boy wanted to ask questions about this daughter of Bob Thorpe's, but a diffidence, for which there was no accounting, held him back. He was curious as he had been whenever he heard of or thought of her, and as he had been when he had once seen her. But somehow he did not care to admit that curiosity even to Jed, and when he tried to analyze the reason for his reticence there was no doing so.

Now came more knowledge of the waste places with weeks of riding; more knowledge of the barren area in his own heart with self-study; more pertinent, that which the Captain typified.

And all the time that struggle continued, which at times seemed only the hopeless floundering of a man in quicksands — life on the river bank so close; death below, certain, mocking his efforts.

"He has faith in himself because he is physically equipped," VB murmured one day as he saw the Captain standing against the sky on a distant ridge. "His belief in himself is justified. But I — what do I know about my own capabilities?"

Yet a latent quality in the boy was the sort that offsets doubts, else why this emulation of the stallion, why this feeling that was almost love, constant, always growing, never hesitating?

Like most men, Young VB was unprepared for the big moments of his life. Could we only foresee them, is the plaint of men! Could we only know and go out to meet them in spirit proper! And yet that very state of preparation might take from the all-encompassing grandeur of those passages a potent element.

After all, this scheme of things has its compensations, and inability to foretell the future may be one of the greatest.

With fear in his heart and black discouragement and lack of faith, Young VB went out to meet what proved to be his first great moment.

Jed had gone to the railroad, bound for the Springs, to untangle a mess of red tape that had snarled about his filing on some land. VB was left alone, and for days the young fellow saw no one. In the natural loneliness that followed, the assault came upon him with manifold force. He could not sleep, could not eat, could not remain in one place or keep his mind on a fixed purpose.

He walked about, talking to himself in the silence, trying ineffectually to do the necessary work of the ranch, trying to stifle the loud voice that begged him to forego all the struggle and let his impulses carry him where they would.

But were not his impulses carrying him? Was it not his first impulse to go on with the fight? He did not think of that.

At times it was hard indeed to differentiate between the real and the unreal. The voice that wheedled was such a twister of words and terms, and its ally, the thirst, raged with such virility that he was forced to do something with his body. To remain an unresisting victim to the torture would only invite disaster.

Throwing a saddle on his "top" horse, Young VB set out, leaving the half-prepared dinner as it was, unable even to wait for food. He rode swiftly up the gulch to where it forked, and then to the right, letting the stanch animal under him cover the ground at a swinging trot. In three hours he was miles from the ranch, far back in the hills, and climbing to the top of a stretching ridge. He breathed through his mouth, to let the air on his burning throat, and twisted his bridle reins until the stout leather was misshapen, utterly lost in the conflict which went on within, heedless of all else.

Suddenly he realized that his horse had come a long distance without rest. He dismounted in a thicket of cedars, sharply repentant that his own torment had led him to forget the beast that served him, and even the distraction of that concern brought relief.

With the cinch eased the horse stood and breathed gratefully. But he was not fagged, he was still alert and eager. His ears were set stiffly forward, and he gazed upwind, sniffing softly now and then.

"What you see, cayuse?" VB asked, trying to make out the cause of that attentiveness.

Again the sniffing, and of a sudden the horse froze, stopped his breathing, and VB, a hand on the beast's hip, felt a quick tremor run through him.

Then the man saw that which had caused the animal to tremble, and the sight set him tingling just as it always did.

A hundred yards up the ridge, sharp against the sky, commanding, watchful, stood the Captain. He had not seen or scented VB, for he looked in other directions, moving his head from point to point, scanning every nook of the country below him. Something mannish there was about that beast, a comprehensive, planned vigilance. Down below him in a sag fed the mares.

As VB looked at that watcher he felt the lust to possess crawling up, surging through him, blotting out that other desire, that torment, making his breath congest, making his mouth dry. He tightened his cinch and mounted.

The Captain did not see VB until the rider came clear of the cover in which he had halted.

For the instant only, as the rushing horseman broke through the cedars, a scudding, fluttering object hurtling across the low brush, the black stallion stood as though his feet were imbedded in the rock under him, his head full toward the rushing rider, nose up, astonishment in the very angle of his stiff ears. Then those ears went flat; the sleek body pivoted on its dainty hind feet, and a scream of angered warning came from the long throat.

Even as the Captain's front hoofs clawed the ground in his first leap, the mares were running. They drew close together, frightened by the abruptness of the alarm, scuttling away from the punishment they knew would be coming from their master if they wasted seconds.

VB was possessed again. His reason told him that a single horseman had no chance in the world with that bunch, that he could not hope to keep up even long enough to scatter the band, that he would only run his mount down, good horse that he was. But the lust urged him on, tugging at his vitals, and he gave vent to his excitement in sharp screams of joy, the joy of the hunt — and the joy of honest attempt at supreme accomplishment.

The dust trailed behind the bunch, enveloping the rushing Captain in a dun mantle, finally to be whipped away by the breeze. They tore down stiff sagebrush in their flight; and so great was the strain that their bellies skimmed incredibly close to the ground.

VB's horse caught the spirit of the chase, as do all animals when they follow their kind. He extended himself to the last fiber, and with astonishment — a glad astonishment that brought a whoop of triumph — the boy saw that the mares were not drawing away — that he was crawling up on them!

But the Captain! Ah, he was running away from the man who gave chase, was putting more distance between them at every thundering leap, was drawing closer to his slower mares, lip stretched back over his gleaming teeth, jaws working as he strained to reach them and make that band go still faster.

VB's quirt commenced to sing its goading tune,

slashing first on one side, then on the other. He hung far forward over the fork of his saddle, leaning low to offer the least possible resistance to the wind. Now and then he called aloud to his pony, swearing with glad savagery.

The Captain reached his bunch, closing in on them with a burst of speed that seemed beyond the abilities of blood and bone. The man behind thought he heard those long teeth pop as they caught the rump of a scurrying mare; surely he heard the stallion's scream of rage as, after nipping mare after mare, running to and fro behind them, he found that they had opened their hearts to the last limit and could go no faster. They *could not* do it — and the rider behind was crawling up, jump for jump, gaining a yard, losing a foot, gaining again, steadily, relentlessly.

VB did not know that Kelly, the horse buyer, and one of Dick Worth's riders had given the outlaws a long, tedious race that morning as they were coming in from the dry country to the west for water and better feed. He did not know that the band had been filling their bellies with great quantities of water, crowding them still more with grasses, until there was no room left for the working of lungs, for the stretching of taxed muscles.

He saw only the one fact: that he was gaining on the Captain. He did not stop even to consider the obvious ending of such a chase. He might scatter the band, but what of it? When the last hope had been cast the Captain would strike out alone, would turn all the energy that now went to driving his mares to making good his own escape, and then there would be no more race — just a widening of a breach that could not be closed.

But VB did not think of anything beyond the next stride. His mind was possessed with the idea that every leap of the laboring beast under him must bring him closer to the huddle of frantic horses, nearer to the flying hindquarters of the jet leader who tried so hard to make his authority override circumstance.

The slashing of the quirt became more vicious. VB strained farther forward. His lips were parted, his eyes strained open with excitement, and the tears started by that rushing streamed over his cheeks.

"E-e-eyah!" he shrieked.

The buckskin mare found a hole. Her hind legs went into the air, sticking toward the sky above that thundering clump of tossing, rushing bodies with its fringes of fluttering hair. Her legs seemed to poise a moment; then they went down slowly. The Captain leaped her prostrate body, to sink his teeth into the flank of a sorrel that lagged half a length behind the others.

VB passed so near the buckskin as she gained her faltering feet that he could have slashed her with his quirt. Yet he had no eyes for her, had no heed for any of the mares. He was playing for the bigger game.

The sorrel quit, unable to respond to that punishment, fearful of her master. She angled off to the right, to be rid of him, and disappeared through a clump of trees. The stallion shrilled his anger and disgust, slowing his gallop a half-dozen jumps as though he wanted to follow and punish her cruelly.

Then he glanced backward, threw his nose in the air and, stretching to his own tremendous speed again, stormed on.

The huddle of mares became less compact, seemed to lose also its unity of purpose. The Captain had more to do. His trips from flank to flank of the band were longer. By the time he had spurred the gray at the left back into the lead the brown three-year-old on the other wing was a loiterer by a length. Then, when she was sent ahead, the gray was lagging again. And another by her side, perhaps.

"E-e-eyah!"

VB's throat was raw from the screaming, but he did not know it — no more than he knew that his hat was gone or that his nerves still yearned for their stinging stimulant.

The cry, coming again and again, worried the Captain. Each time it crackled from VB's lips the black nose was flung high and an eye which glared orange hate even at that distance rolled back to watch this yelling pursuer.

VB saw, and began to shout words at the animal, to cry his challenge, to curse.

The galloping gray quit, without an attempt to rally. The Captain brought to bear a terrific punishment, dropping back to within thirty yards of the man who pressed him, but it was useless, for she was spent. The water and luscious grass in her dammed up the reservoirs of her vitality, would not let her respond. When the stallion gave her up and tore on after the others she dropped even her floundering gallop, and as VB raced past her he heard the breath sob down her throat.

On and across they tore, dropping into sags of the ridge, climbing sharp little pitches, swinging now to the right and bending back to the left again in a sweeping curve. The uneven galloping of the horse under him, the gulps for breath the pony made as the footing fooled him and he jolted sharply, the shiftings and duckings and quick turnings as they stormed through groups of trees, the rattle of brush as it smote his boot toes and stirrups were all unheeded by VB.

Once his shoulder met a tough cedar bough, and the blow wrenched it from its trunk. His face was whipped to rawness by smaller branches, and one knee throbbed dully where it had skimmed a bowlder as they shot past. But he saw only that floundering band ahead.

The buckskin was gone, the sorrel, the gray; next, two mares quit together, and the Captain, seeing them go, did not slacken his speed, did not even scream his rage. Only four remained, and he gambled on them as against the slight chance of recovering any of those others; for that screaming rider was closing in on him all the time.

Oh, water and grass! How necessary both are to life, but how dangerous at a time like this! Pop-pop! The teeth closed on those running hips. The vainness of it all! They could go no faster. They had tried first from instinct, then from willingness; now they tried from fear as their lord tortured them. But though the will was there, the ability could not come, not even when the Captain pushed through them, and in a desperate maneuver set the pace, showing them his fine heels and clean limbs, demonstrating how easy it was to go on and on and draw away from that rider who tugged at his muffler that wind might find and cool his throat, burning now from unalloyed hope.

And so VB, the newest horse runner on the range, scattered the Captain's band, accomplishing all that the best of the men who rode that country had ever been able to boast.

The stallion tried once more to rally his mates into escape, but their hearts were bursting, their lungs clogged. They could do no more.

Then away he went alone, head high and turning from side to side, mane flaunting, tail trailing gracefully behind him, beauty in every regal line and curve, majestic superiority in each stride he took.

He raced off into the country that stretched eastward, the loser for the time of one set of conquests but free — free to go on and make himself more high, more powerful, more a thing to be emulated even by man.

He ran lightly, evenly, without effort, and the gap between him and the rider behind, narrowed by such tremendous exertion from that lathered pony, widened with scarce an added effort.

But VB went on, driving his reeking pony mercilessly. He had ceased yelling now. His face was set; blood that had been whipped into it by his frenzy, by the rushing of the wind, by the smiting of branches, left the skin. It became white, and from that visage two eyes glowed abnormally brilliant. For the Captain was taking off the ridge where it bent and struck into the north, was plunging down over the pitch into the shadows. He was going his best, in long, keen strides that would carry him to the bottom with a momentum so tremendous that on the flat he would be running himself into a blur. And VB's face was colorless, with eyes brilliant, because he knew that along the bottom of the drop ran the new drift fence that Bob Thorpe's men were erecting.

He began to plead with his pony, to talk to him childishly, to beg him to keep his feet, to coax him to last, to pray him to follow — and in control of himself, and on time! As they dropped off the ridge, down through the sliding shale and scattered brush, VB's right hand, upraised to keep his balance, held the loop of his rope, and the other, flung behind the cantle of his saddle, grasped the coils of the sturdy hemp.

Oh, Captain, your speed was against you! You took off that ridge with those ground-covering leaps, limbs flying, heart set on reaching the bottom with a swirl of speed that would dishearten your follower. But you did not reckon on an obstruction, on the thing your eyes encountered when halfway down that height and going with all the power within you. Those fresh posts and the wires strung between them! A fence! Men had invaded your territory with their barriers, and at such a time! You knew, too, that there was no jumping it; they had set the posts so far up on the pitch that no take-off had been left.

So the Captain tried to stop. With haunches far under him, front feet straight before, belly scrubbing the brush, he battled to overcome the awful impetus his body had received up above. Sprawling, sliding, feet shooting in any direction as the footing gave, he struggled to stop his progress. It was no simple matter; indeed, checking that flight was far more difficult than the attaining of that speed. In the midst of rolling, bounding stones, sliding dust, breaking brush, the great stallion gradually slowed his going. Slow and more slowly he went on toward the bottom; almost stopped, but still was unable to bring his muscles into play for a dash to right or left

PURSUIT

On behind, pony floundering in the wake of the Captain, rode VB, right hand high, snapping back and forth to hold him erect, rope dangling from it crazily. He breathed through his mouth, and at every exhalation his vocal chords vibrated.

Perhaps even then the Captain might have won. The odds of the game were all against him, it is true, for breaking down the pitch as he did, it required longer for him to reach the bottom in possession of his equilibrium than it did the slower-moving horse that bore VB. It would have been a tight squeeze for the horse, but the man was in a poor position to cast his loop with any degree of accuracy.

But a flat sliding stone discounted all other factors. Nothing else mattered. The Captain came to a stop, eyes wild, ears back. With a slow-starting, mighty lunge, he made as though to turn and race down along the line of fence before VB could get within striking distance. The great muscles contracted, his ragged hoofs sought a hold. The hind legs straightened, that mighty force bore on his footing — and the stone slipped! The Captain was outlucked.

His hind legs shot backward, staggering him. His hindquarters slipped downhill, throwing his head up to confront VB. His nostrils flared, that orange hate in his eyes met the glow from his pursuer's, who came down upon him — only half a dozen lengths away!

CHAPTER X

CAPTURE

IT does not take a horse that is bearing a rider downhill an appreciable length of time to take one more stride. Gravity does the work. The horse jerks his fore legs from under his body and then shoots them out again for fresh hold to keep his downward progress within reason.

VB's pony went down the drop with much more rapidity than safety, in short, jerky, stiff-legged plunges, hindquarters scrooged far under his body; alert, watching his footing, grunting in his care not to take too great risks.

When the Captain, fooled by false footing, was whirled about to face the down-coming rider, the pony's fore feet had just drawn themselves out of the way to let his body farther down the slope. And when the sturdy legs again shot out to strike rock and keep horse and VB upright, the black stallion had started to wheel. But in the split second which intervened between the beginning and ending of that floundering jump, eyes met eyes. The eyes of a man met the eyes of a beast, and heart read heart. The eyes of a man who had frittered his life, who had flaunted his heritage of strength in body and bone until he had become a weakling, a cringing, whining center of abnormal nervous activities, fearing himself, met the eyes of a beast that knew himself to be a paragon of his kind, the final achievement of his strain, a commanding force that had never been curbed, that had defied alike his own kingdom and the race from which had sprung the being now confronting him.

The eyes of him who had been a weakling met the eyes of that which had been superstrong and without a waver; they held, they penetrated, and, suddenly born from the purposeless life of Danny Lenox, flamed Young VB's soul. All the emulation, all the lust this beast before him had roused in his heart, became amalgamated with that part of him which subtly strove to drag him away from debauchery, and upon those blending elements of strength was set the lasting stamp of his individuality.

His purpose flamed in his eyes and its light was so great that the horse read, and, reading, set his ears forward and screamed — not so much a scream of anger as of wondering terror. For the beast caught the significance of that splendid determination which made for conquest with a power equal to his own strength, which was making for escape. The telepathic communication from the one to the other was the same force that sends a jungle king into antics at the pleasure of his trainer — the language that transcends species!

The pony's hoofs dug shale once more, and the

upraised right arm whipped about the tousled head. The rope swished angrily as it slashed the air. Once it circled — and the Captain jumped, lunging off to the left. Twice it cut its disk — and the stallion's quivering flanks gathered for a second leap. It writhed; it stretched out waveringly, seekingly, feelingly as though uncertain, almost blindly, but swiftly — so swiftly! The loop flattened and spread and undulated, drawing the long stretch of hemp after it teasingly. It stopped, as though suddenly tired. It poised with uncanny deliberation. Then, as gently as a maiden's sigh, it settled — settled — drooped — and the Captain's nose, reaching out for liberty, to be free of this man whose eyes flamed a determination so stanch that it went down to his beast heart, thrust itself plumb through the middle.

The hoarse rip of the hard-twist coming through its hondu, the whistle of breath from the man's tight teeth, the rattle of stone on stone; then the squeal from the stallion as for the first time in his life a bond tightened on him!

He shook his head angrily, and even as he leaped a third time back toward his free hills one forefoot was raised to strike from him the snaring strand. The pawing hoof did not reach its mark, did not find the thin, lithe thing which throttled down on him, for the Captain's momentum carried him to the end of the rope.

They put the strain on the hemp, both going

CAPTURE

away, those horses. VB struggled with his mount to have him ready for the shock, but before he could bring about a full stop that shock arrived. It seemed as though it would tear the horn from the saddle. The pony, sturdy little beast, was yanked to his knees and swung half about, and VB recovered himself only by grabbing the saddle fork.

The black stallion again faced the man — faced him because his heels had been cracked in a semicircle through the air by the force of that burning thing about his neck. For ten long seconds the Captain stood braced against the rope, moving his head slowly from side to side for all the world as a refractory, gentled colt might do, with as much display of fight as would be shown by a mule that dissented at the idea of being led across a ditch. He just stood there stupidly, twisting his head.

The thick mane rumpled up under the tightening rope, some of the drenched hair of the neck was pulled out as the hemp rolled upward, drawing closer, shutting down and down. The depression in the flesh grew deeper. One hind foot lost its hold in the shale and shot out; the Captain lifted it and moved it forward again slowly, cautiously, for fresh, steady straining.

Then it came. The windpipe closed; he coughed, and like the sudden fury of a mountain thunderstorm the Captain turned loose his giant forces. The thing had jerked him back in his rush toward freedom. It held him where he did not want to be held! And it choked!

Forefeet clawing, rearing to his hind legs with a quivering strength of lift that dragged the bracing pony through the shale, the great, black horse-regal screamed and coughed his rage and beat upon that vibrating strand which made him prisoner — that web — that fragile thing!

Again and again he struck it, but it only danced — only danced, and tightened its clutch on his throat! He reached for it with his long teeth and clamped them on it, but the thing would not yield. He settled to all fours again, threw his head from side to side, and strove to move backward with a frenzied floundering that sent the pebbles rattling yards about him.

It was a noble effort. Into the attempt to drag away from that anchorage the Captain put his very spirit. He struggled and choked and strained. And all the time that man sat there on his horse, tense, watching silently, moving his free hand slightly to and fro, as though beating time to music. His lips were parted, his face still blanched. And in his eyes glowed that purpose which knows no defeat!

System departed. Like a hot blast wickedness came. Teeth bared, ears flat, with sounds like an angered child's ranting coming from his throat, the stallion charged his man enemy just as he had charged the powerful Percheron who had come to challenge him a month ago. The

CAPTURE

saddle horse, seeing it, avoided the brunt of the first blind rush, taking the Captain's shoulder on his rump as the black hurtler went past, striking thin air.

VB felt the Captain's breath, saw from close up the lurid flame in his eyes, sensed the power of those teeth, the sledge-hammer force behind those untrimmed hoofs. And he came alive, the blood shooting close under his skin again and making the gray face bronze, then deeper than bronze. His eyes puffed under the stress of that emotion, and he felt a primitive desire to growl as the Captain whirled and came again. It was man to beast, and somewhere down yonder through the generations a dead racial memory came back and Young VB, girded for the conflict, ached to have his forest foe in reach, to have the fight run high, to have his chance to dare and do in fleshly struggle!

It was not long in coming. The near hoof, striking down to crush his chest, fell short, and the hair of VB's chap leg went ripping from the leather, while along his thigh crept a dull, spreading ache.

He did not notice that, though, for he was raised in his stirrups, right hand lifted high, its fingers clutched about the lash of his loaded quirt. He felt the breath again, hot, wet, and a splatter of froth from the flapping lips struck his cheek. Then the right hand came down with a snap and a jerk, with all the vigor of muscular force that VB could summon.

His eye had been good, his judgment true. The Captain's teeth did not sink into his flesh, for the quirt-butt, a leaden slug, crunched on the horse's skull, right between the ears!

The fury of motion departed, like the going of a cyclone. The Captain dropped to all fours and hung his head, staggered a half-dozen short paces drunkenly, and then sighed deeply —

He reached the end of the rope. It came tight again, and with the tightening — the battle! Thrice more he charged the man with all the hate his wild heart could summon, but not once did those dreadful teeth find that which they sought. Again the front hoof met its mark and racked the flesh of VB's leg, but that did not matter. He could stand that punishment, for he was winning! He was countering the stallion's efforts, which made the contest an even break; and his rope was on and he had dealt one telling blow with his quirt. Two points! And the boy screamed his triumph as the missile he swung landed again, on the soft nose this time, the nose so wrinkled with hateful desire — and the Captain swung off to one side from the stinging force of it.

Not in delight at punishment was that cry. The blow on the skull, the slug at the nose stabbed VB to his tenderest depths. But he knew it must be so, and his shout was a shout of conquest — of the first man asserting primal authority, of the last man coming into his own!

CAPTURE

The dust they stirred rose stiflingly. Down there under the hill no moving breath of air would carry it off. The pony under VB grunted and strained, but was jerked sharply about by the rushes of the heavier stallion, heavier and built of things above mere flesh and bone and tendon. The Captain's belly dripped water; VB's face was glossy with it, his hair plastered down to brow and temple.

The three became tired. In desperation the Captain dropped the fight, turned to run, plunged out as though to part the strands. VB's heart leaped as his faith in the rope faltered — but it held, and the stallion, pulled about, lost his footing, floundered, stumbled, went down, and rolled into the shale, feet threshing the air.

It was an opening — the widest VB had had, wider than he could have hoped for, and he rushed in, stabbing his horse shamelessly with spurs and babbling witlessly as he strove to make slack in the rope. The slack came. Then the quick jerk of the wrist — the trick he had pertected back there in Jed's corral — and a potential half-hitch traveled down the rope.

The Captain floundered to get his feet under him, and the loop in the rope dissolved. Again the wrist twitch, again the shooting loop and —

"Scotched!" screamed Young VB. "Scotched! You're my property!"

Scotched! The rope had found its hold about the off hind ankle of the soiled stallion, and there it clung in a tight, relentless grasp. The rope from neck to limb was so short that it kept the foot clear of the ground, crippling the Captain. and as the great horse floundered to his feet VB had him powerless. The stallion stood dazed, looking down at the thing which would not let him kick, which would not let him step.

Then he sprang forward, and when the rope came tight he was upended, a shoulder plowing the shale.

"It's no use!" the man cried, his voice crackling in excitement. "I've got you right — right — *right!*"

But the Captain would not quit. He tried even then to rise to his hind legs and make assault, but the effort only sent him falling backward, squealing — and left him on his side, moaning for his gone liberty.

For he knew. He knew that his freedom was gone, even as he made his last floundering, piteous endeavors. He got up and tried to run, but every series of awkward moves only sent his black body down into the dust and dirt, and at last he rested there, head up, defiance still in his eyes, but legs cramped under him.

And then VB wanted to cry. He went through all the sensations — the abrupt drop of spirits, the swelling in the throat, the tickling in the nostrils.

"Oh, Captain!" he moaned. "Captain, don't you see I wouldn't harm you? Only you had to be *mine!* I had to get bigger than you were, Captain — for my own salvation. It was the only way, boy; it was the only way!"

And he sat there for a long time, his eyes without the light of triumph, on his captive.

His heart-beats quickened, a new warmth commenced to steal through his veins, a new faith in self welled up from his innermost depths, making his pulses sharp and hard, making his muscles swell, sending his spirit up and up.

He had fought his first big fight and he had won!

Blood began to drip from the stallion's nose.

"It's where I struck you!" whispered VB, the triumph all gone again, solicitation and a vast love possessing him. "It's where I struck you, Captain. Oh, it hurts me, too — but it must be so, because things are as they are. There will be more hurts, boy, before we're through. But it must be!"

His voice gritted on the last.

Sounds from behind roused VB, and he looked around.

The sunlight was going even from the ridge up there, and the whole land was in shadow. He was a long way from the ranch with this trophy — his, but still ready to do battle at the end of his rope.

"Got one?" a man cried, coming up, and VB recognized him as one of the trio of fence builders, riding back to their camp.

"Yes — one," muttered VB, and turned to look at the Captain.

Then the man cried: "You've got th' Captain!"

"It's the Captain," said VB unsteadily, as though too much breath were in his lungs. "He's mine — you know — mine!"

The others looked at him in silent awe.

CHAPTER XI

A Letter and a Narrative

JED AVERY had been away from Young VB almost two weeks, and he had grown impatient in the interval. So he pushed his bay pony up the trail from Ranger, putting the miles behind him as quickly as possible. The little man had fretted over every step of the journey homeward, and from Colt on into the hills it was a conscious effort that kept him from abusing his horse by overtravel.

"If he should have gone an' busted over while I was away I'd — I'd never forgive myself — lettin' that boy go to th' bad just for a dinky claim!"

It was the thousandth time he had made the declaration, and as he spoke the words a thankfulness rose in his heart because of what he had *not* heard in Ranger. He knew that VB had kept away from town. Surely that was a comfort, an assurance, a justification for his faith that was firm even under the growling.

Still, there might have been a wanderer with a bottle —

And as he came in sight of his own buildings Jed put the pony to a gallop for the first time during that long journey. Smoke rose from the chimney, the door stood open, an atmosphere of habitation was about the place, and that proved something. He crowded his horse close against the gate, leaned low, unfastened the hasp, and rode on through.

"Oh, VB!" he called, and from the cabin came an answering hail, a scraping of chair legs, and the young fellow appeared in the doorway.

"How's th' —"

Jed did not finish the question then — or ever. His eagerness for the meeting, the light of anticipation that had been in his face, disappeared. He reined up his horse with a stout jerk, and for a long moment sat there motionless, eyes on the round corral. Then his shoulders slacked forward and he raised a hand to scratch his chin in bewilderment.

For yonder, his nose resting on one of the gate bars, watching the newcomer, safe in the inclosure, alive, just as though he belonged there, stood the Captain!

After that motionless moment Jed turned his eyes back to Young VB, and stared blankly, almost witlessly. Then he raised a limp hand and half pointed toward the corral, while his lips formed a soundless question.

VB stepped from the doorway and walked toward Jed, smiling.

"Yes," he said with soft pride, as though telling of a sacred thing, "the Captain is there — in our corral."

Jed drew a great breath.

"Did you do it — and alone?"

"Well, there was n't any one else about," VB replied modestly.

Again Jed's chest heaved.

"Well, I'm a—"

He ended in inarticulate distress, searching for a proper expletive, mouth open and ready, should he find one. Then he was off his horse, both hands on the boy's shoulders, looking into the eyes that met his so steadily.

"You done it, Young VB!" he cried brokenly. "You done it! Oh, I'm proud of you! Your old adopted daddy sure is! You done it all by yourself, an' it's somethin' that nobody has ever been able to do before!"

Then they both laughed aloud, eyes still clinging.

"Come over and get acquainted," suggested VB. "He's waiting for us."

They started for the corral, Jed's eyes, now flaming as they took in the detail of that wonderful creature, already seen by him countless times, but now for the first time unfree.

The stallion watched them come, moving his feet up and down uneasily and peering at them between the bars. VB reached for the gate fastening, and the horse was away across the corral, snorting, head up, as though fearful.

"Why, Captain!" the boy cried. "What ails you?"

"What ails him?" cried Jed. "Man alive, I'd expect to see him tryin' to tear our hearts out!"

"Oh, but he's like a woman!" VB said softly, watching the horse as he swung the gate open.

They stepped inside, Jed with caution. VB walked straight across to the horse and laid his hand on the splendid curve of the rump.

"Well, I'm a —" Again Jed could find no proper word to express his astonishment. He simply took off his hat and swung it in one hand, like an embarrassed schoolgirl.

"Come over and meet the boss, Captain," VB laughed, drawing the black head around by its heavy forelock.

And the Captain came — unexpectedly. The boy realized the danger with the first plunge and threw his arms about the animal's neck, crying to him to be still. And Jed realized, too. He slipped outside, putting bars between himself and those savage teeth which reached out for his body.

Foiled, the stallion halted.

"Captain," exclaimed VB, "what ails you?"

"To be sure, nothin' ails him," said Jed sagely. "You're his master; you own him, body and soul; but you ain't drove th' hate for men out of his heart. He seems to love you — but not others — yes —"

His voice died out as he watched the black beast make love to the tall young chap who scolded into his dainty ear. The soft, thin lips plucked at VB's clothing, nuzzling about him as he stood with arms clasped around the glossy neck. The great cheek rubbed against the boy's side until it pushed him from his tracks, though he strained playfully against the pressure. Such was the fierceness of that horse's allegiance. His nostrils fluttered, but no sound came from them: the beast whisperings of affection. All the time VB scolded softly, as a father might banter with a child. And when the boy looked up a great pride was in his face, and Jed understood.

"That's right, Young VB — be proud of it! Be proud that he's yours; be proud that he's yours, an' yours only. Keep him that way; to be sure, an' you've earned it!"

Then he stepped close to the bars and gazed at the animal with the critical look of a connoisseur.

"Not a hair that ain't black," he muttered. "Black from ankle to ear; hoofs almost black, black in th' nostrils. Black horses generally have brown eyes, but you can't even tell where th' pupil is in his!

"Say, VB, he makes th' ace of spades look like new snow, don't he?"

"He does that!" cried VB, and putting his hands on the animal's back, he leaped lightly up, sitting sidewise on the broad hips and playing with the heavy tail.

"VB, I'm a — Lord, a thousand dollars for a new oath!"

At VB's suggestion they started back to the cabin.

"Why, boy, you're limpin'!" the old man exclaimed. "An' in both legs!" He stopped and looked the young fellow over from hat to heel. "One side of your face's all skinned. Looks as though your left hand'd all been smashed up, it's that swelled. You move like your back hurt, too — like sin. VB?"

The boy stopped and looked down at the ground. Then his eyes met those of the old rancher, and Jed Avery understood — he had seen the bond between man and horse; he realized what must have transpired between them.

And he knew the love that men can have for animals, something which, if you have never felt it, is far beyond comprehension. So he asked just this question: "How long?"

And VB answered: "Six days — from dawn till dark. One to get a halter on him, another to get my hand on his head; three days in the Scotch hobble, and the last — to ride him like a hand-raised colt."

Jed replaced his hat, pulling it low to hide his eyes.

"Ain't I proud to be your daddy?" he whispered.

An overwhelming pride — a pride raised to the nth degree, of the sort that is above the understanding of most men — was in the tone *timbre* of the question.

They went on into the house.

"Jed," VB said, as though he had waited to broach something of great import, "I've written a letter this morning, and I want to read it to you, just to see how it sounds out loud."

He sat down in a chair and drew sheets of small tablet paper toward him.

Jed, without answer, leaned against the table and waited. VB read:

"MY DEAR FATHER:

"I am writing merely to say that I know you were right and I was wrong.

"I am in a new life, where men do big, real things which justify their own existence. I am finding myself. I am getting that perspective which lets me see just how right you were and how wrong I was.

"Since coming here I have done something real. I have captured and made mine the wildest horse that ever ran these hills. I am frankly proud of it. I may live to do things of more obvious greatness, but that will be because men have had their sense of values warped. For me, this attainment is a true triumph.

"I am now in the process of taming another beast, more savage than the one I have mastered, and possessing none of his noble qualities. It is a beast not of the sort we can grapple with, though we can see it in men. It is giving me a hard battle, but try to believe that my efforts are sincere and, though it may take my whole lifetime, I am bound to win in the end.

"This letter will be mailed in Kansas City by a friend. I am many days' travel from that point. When I am sure of the other victory I shall let you know where I am.

"Your affectionate son,"

He tossed the sheets back to the table top.

"I'm going to get it over to Ant Creek and let some of the boys take it to the river when they go with beef," he explained. "Now, how does it sound?"

"Fine, VB, fine!" Jed muttered, rubbing one cheek. "To be sure, it ain't so much what you say as th' way you say it — makin' a party feel as though you meant it from th' bottom of your feet to th' tip of th' longest hair on your head!"

"Well, Jed, I do mean it just that way. That horse out there — he — he stands for so much now. He stands for everything I have n't been, and for all that I want to be. He ran free as the birds, but it could n't always be so. He had to succumb, had to give up that sort of liberty.

"I took his power from him, made him my own, made him my servant. Yet it did n't scathe his spirit. It has changed all that bitterness into love, all that wasted energy into doing something useful. I did n't break him, Jed; I converted him. Understand?"

"I do, VB; but we won't convert this here other beast. We'll bust him wide open, won't we? Break him, body an' spirit!"

The boy smiled wanly.

"That's what we're trying to do."

He pointed to the candle in its daubed bottle.

"Just to keep the light burning, Jed — just to keep its light fighting back the darkness. The little flame of that candle breaks the power of the black thing which would shut it in — like a heart being good and true in spite of the rotten body in which it beats. And when my body commences to want the old things — to want them, oh, so badly — I just think of this little candle here, calm and quiet and steady, sticking out of what was once a cesspool, a poison pot, and making a place in the night where men can see."

While a hundred could have been counted slowly they remained motionless, quiet, not a sound breaking the silence.

Then Jed began talking in a half-tone:

"I know, Young VB; I know. You've got time now to light it and nurse th' flame up so's it won't need watchin' — an' not miss things that go by in th' dark. Some of us puts it off too long — like a man I know — now. I didn't know him then — when it happened. He was wanderin' around in a night that never turned to day, thinkin' he knowed where he was goin', but all th' time just bein' fooled by th' dark.

"And there was a girl back in Kansas. He started after her, but it was so dark he couldn't find th' way, an' when he did —

"Some folks is fools enough to say women don't die of broken hearts. But — well, when a feller knows some things he wants to go tell 'em to men who don't know; to help 'em to understand, if he can; to give 'em a hand if they do see but can't find their way out —"

He stopped, staring at the floor. VB had no cause to search for identities.

From the corral came a shrill, prolonged neighing. VB arose and laid a hand gently on Jed's bowed shoulder.

"That's the Captain," he said solemnly; "and he calls me when he's thirsty."

While he was gone Jed remained as he had been left, staring at the floor.

CHAPTER XII

WOMAN WANTS

GAIL THORPE rose from the piano in the big ranch house of the S Bar S, rearranged the mountain flowers that filled a vase on a tabouret, then knocked slowly, firmly, commandingly, on a door that led from the living room.

"Well, I don't want you; but I s'pose you might as well come in and get it off your mind!"

The voice from the other side spoke in feigned annoyance. It continued to grumble until a lithe figure, topped by a mass of hair like pulled sunshine, flung itself at him, twining warm arms about his neck and kissing the words from the lips of big Bob Thorpe as he sat before his desk in the room that served as the ranch office.

"Will you ever say it again — that you don't want me?" she demanded.

"No — but merely because I'm intimidated into promising," he answered. His big arms went tight about the slender body and he pulled his daughter up on his lap.

A silence, while she fussed with his necktie. Her blue eyes looked into his gray ones a moment as though absently, then back to the necktie. Her fingers fell idle; her head snuggled against his neck. Bob Thorpe laughed loud and long.

"Well, what is it this morning?" he asked between chuckles.

The girl sat up suddenly, pushed back the hair that defied fastenings, and tapped a stretched palm with the stiff forefinger of the other hand.

"I'm not a Western girl," she declared deliberately; and then, as the brown face before her clouded, hastened: "Oh, I'm not wanting to go away! I mean, I'm not truly a Western girl, but I want to be. I want to fit better.

"When we decided that I should graduate and come back here with my mommy and daddy for the rest of my life, I decided. There was nothing halfway about it. Some of the other girls thought it awful; but I don't see the attraction in their way of living.

"When I was a little girl I was a sort of tom-cow-boy. I could do things as well as any of the boys I ever knew could do them. But after ten years, mostly away in the East, where girls are like plants, I've lost it all. Now I want to get it back."

"Well, go to it!"

"Wait! I want to start well — high up. I want to have the best that there is to have. I — want — a — horse!"

"Horse? Bless me, *bambino*, there are fifty broken horses running in the back pasture now, besides what the boys have on the ride. Take your pick!"

"Oh, I know!" she said with gentle scoffing.

"*That* sort of a horse — just cow-ponies. I love 'em, but I guess — well —"

"You've been educated away from 'em, you mean?" he chuckled.

"Well, whatever it is — I want something better. I, as a daughter of the biggest, best man in Colorado, want to ride the best animal that ever felt a cinch."

"Well?"

"And I want to have him now, so I can get used to him this fall and look forward to coming back to him in the spring."

Bob Thorpe took both her hands in one of his.

"And if a thing like that will make my *bambino* happy, I guess she'll have it."

The girl kissed him and held her cheek close against his for a breath.

"When I go to Denver for the stock show I'll pick the best blue ribbon —"

"Denver!" she exclaimed indignantly, sitting straight and tossing her head. "I want a real horse — a horse bred and raised in these mountains — a horse I can trust. None of your blue-blooded stock. They're like the girls I went to college with!"

Bob Thorpe let his laughter roll out.

"Well, what do you expect to find around here? Have you seen anything you like?"

She pulled her hands from his grasp and stretched his mouth out of shape with her little fingers until he squirmed.

"No, I have n't seen him; but I've heard the cowboys talking. Over at Mr. Avery's ranch they've caught a black horse —"

Bob Thorpe set her suddenly up on the arm of his chair and shook her soundly.

"Look here, young lady!" he exclaimed. "You're dreaming! I know what horse you're talking about. He's a wild devil that has run these hills for years. I heard he'd been caught. Get the notion of having him out of your head. I've never seen him but once, and then he was away off; but I've heard tales of him. Why —

"Nonsense! In the first place, he could n't be broken to ride. Men are n't made big enough to break the spirit of a devil like that! They're bigger than humans. So we can end this discussion in peace. It's impossible!"

"All right," Gail said sweetly. "I just let you go on and get yourself into a corner. You don't know what you're talking about. He *has* been ridden. So there! I want him!"

He thrust her to one side, rose, and commenced to pace the room, gesticulating wildly. But it all came to the invariable end of such discussions, and twenty minutes later Gail Thorpe, her smoking, smiling dad at her side, piloted the big touring car down the road, bound for Jed Avery's ranch.

Young VB sat on a box behind the cabin working with a boot-heel that insisted on running over.

He lifted the boot, held it before his face, and squinted one eye to sight the effect of his work — then started at a cry from the road.

The boot still in his hands, VB stopped squinting to listen. Undoubtedly whoever it was wanted Jed; but Jed was away with the horse buyer, looking over his young stuff. So Young VB, boot in hand, its foot clad in a service-worn sock, made his uneven way around the house to make any necessary explanations.

"That must be he!"

The light, high voice of the girl gave the cry just as VB turned the corner and came in sight, and her hand, half extended to point toward the corral, pointed directly into the face of the young man.

He did not hear what she had said, did not venture a greeting. He merely stood and stared at her, utterly without poise. In a crimson flash he realized that this was Gail Thorpe, that she was pretty, and that his bootless foot was covered by a sock that had given way before the stress of walking in high heels, allowing his great toe, with two of its lesser conspirators, to protrude. To his confusion, those toes seemed to be swelling and for the life of him he could make them do nothing but stand stiffly in the air almost at right angles with the foot.

His breeding cried out for a retreat, for a leap into shelter; but his wits had lost all grace. He lifted the half-naked foot and carefully brushed the dirt from the sock. Then, leaning a shoulder against the corner of the cabin, he drew the boot on. Stamping it to the ground to settle his foot into place, he said, "Good morning," weakly and devoid of heartiness.

Bob Thorpe had not noticed this confusion, for his eyes were on the corral. But Gail, a peculiar twinkle in her eyes, had seen it all — and with quick intuition knew that it was something more than the embarrassment of a cow-puncher — and struggled to suppress her smiles.

"Good afternoon," Thorpe corrected. "Jed here?"

"No; he's riding," VB answered.

The cattleman moved a pace to the left and tilted his head to see better the Captain, who stormed around and around the corral, raising a great dust.

"We came over to look at a horse I heard was here — this one, I guess. Isn't he the wild stallion?"

"Used to be wild."

"He looks it yet. Watch him plunge!" Thorpe cried.

"He's never seen an automobile before," VB explained, as the three moved nearer the corral.

The horse was frightened. He quivered when he stood in one place, and the quivering always grew more violent until it ended in a plunge. He rose to his hind legs, head always toward the car, and pawed the air; then settled back and ran to the far side of the inclosure, with eyes for nothing but that machine.

They halted by the bars, Thorpe and his daughter standing close together, Young VB nearer the gate. The boy said something to the horse and laughed softly.

"Why, look, daddy," the girl cried, "he's beginning to calm down!"

The Captain stopped his antics and, still trembling, moved gingerly to the bars. Twice he threw up his head, looked at the machine, and breathed loudly, and once a quick tremor ran through his fine limbs, but the terror was no longer on him.

Bob Thorpe turned a slow gaze on VB. The girl stood with lips parted. A flush came under her fine skin and she clasped her hands at her breast.

"Oh, daddy, what a horse!" she breathed.

And Bob Thorpe echoed: "Lord, what a horse! Anybody tried to ride him?" he asked a moment later.

"He gets work every day," VB answered.

"*Work?* Don't tell me you work that animal!"

The young chap nodded. "Yes; he works right along."

The Captain snorted oudly and tore away in a proud circle of the corral, as though to flaunt his graces.

"Oh, daddy, it took a *man* to break that animal!" the girl breathed.

The bronze of VB's face darkened, then paled. He turned a steady look on the sunny-haired woman, and the full thanks that swelled in his throat almost found words. He wanted to cry out to her, to tell her what such things meant; for she was of his sort, highly bred, capable of understanding. And he found himself thinking: "You are! You are! You're as I thought you must be!"

Then he felt Thorpe's gaze and turned to meet it, a trifle guiltily.

"Yours?" the man asked.

"Mine."

Thorpe turned back to the Captain. Gail drew a quick breath and turned away from him — to the man.

"I thought so when he commenced to quiet," muttered Thorpe.

He looked then at his daughter and found her standing still, hands clasped, lips the least trifle parted, gazing at Young VB.

Something in him urged a quick step forward. It was an alarm, something primal in the fathers of women. But Bob Thorpe put the notion aside as foolishness — or tenderness — and walked closer to the corral, chewing his cigar speculatively. The stallion wrinkled his nose and dropped the ears flat, the orange glimmer coming into his eyes.

"Don't like strangers, I see."

"Not crazy about them," VB answered.

Thorpe walked off to the left, then came back. He removed his cigar and looked at Gail. She fussed with her rebellious hair and her face was flushed; she no longer looked at the horse — or at VB. He felt a curiosity about that flush.

"Well, want to get rid of him?"

Thorpe hooked his thumbs in his vest armholes and confronted VB.

No answer.

"What do you want for him?"

The young fellow started.

"What?" he said in surprise. "I was thinking. I didn't catch your question."

The fact was, he had heard, but had distrusted the sense. The idea of men offering money for the Captain had never occurred to him.

"What do you want for him?"

VB smiled.

"What do I want for him?" he repeated. "I want — feed and water for the rest of his life; shelter when he needs it; the will to treat him as he should be treated. And I guess that's about all."

The other again removed his cigar, and his jaw dropped. A cow-puncher talking so! He could not believe it; and the idea so confused him that he blundered right on with the bargaining. "Five hundred? Seven-fifty? No? Well, how much?"

VB smiled again, just an indulgent smile prompted by the knowledge that he possessed a thing beyond the power of even this man's wealth.

"The Captain is not for sale," he said. "Not to-day — or ever. That's final."

There was more talk, but all the kindly bluffness, all the desire instinctive in Bob Thorpe to give the other man an even break in the bargain, fell flat. This stranger, this thirty-five-dollar-a-month ranch hand, shed his offers as a tin roof sheds rain and with a self-possession characterized by unmistakable assurance.

"Tell Jed I was over," the big man said as they gave up their errand and turned to go. "And" — as he set a foot on the running board of his car — "any time you're our way drop in."

"Yes, do!" added the girl, and her father could not check the impulse which made him turn halfway as though to shut her off.

CHAPTER XIII
VB Fights

JED returned that evening, worn by a hard day's riding. He was silent. VB, too, was quiet and they spoke little until the housework was finished and Jed had drawn off his boots preparatory to turning in.

Then VB said: "Bob Thorpe was over to-day."

"So?"

"Uh-huh; wanted to buy the Captain."

After a pause Jed commented: "That's natural."

"Wanted me to give you the good word."

The old man walked through the doorway into the little bunk room and VB heard him flop into the crude bed.

A short interval of silence.

"Jed," called VB, "ever hear where his daughter went to school?"

A long yawn. Then:

"Yep — don't remember."

Another pause.

"She was over, too."

"Oh-ho-o-o!"

The boy felt himself flushing, and then sat bolt upright, wondering soberly and seriously why it should be so — without reason.

Young VB slept restlessly that night. He tossed and dreamed, waking frequently under a sense of nervous tension, then falling back to half-slumber once more. Thorpe came, and his daughter, offering fabulous sums for the Captain, which were stubbornly refused.

Then, shouting at the top of her voice, the girl cried:

"But I will give you kisses for him! Surely that is enough!"

And VB came back to himself, sitting up in bed and wadding the blankets in his hands. He blinked in the darkness and herded his scattered senses with difficulty. Then the hands left off twisting the covers and went slowly to his throat. For the thirst was on him and in the morning he rose in the grip of the same stifling desire, and his quavering hands spilled things as he ate.

Jed noticed, but made no comment. When the meal was finished he said:

"S'pose I could get you to crawl up on the Captain an' take a shoot up Curley Gulch with an eye out for that black mare an' her yearlin'?"

VB was glad to be alone with his horse, and as he walked to the corral, his bridle over his arm, he felt as though, much as Jed could help him, he could never bring the inspiration which the black beast offered.

He opened the gate and let it swing wide. The Captain came across to him with soft nickerings, deserting the alfalfa he was munching.

He thrust his muzzle into the crook of VB's elbow, and the arm tightened on it desperately, while the other hand went up to twine fingers in the luxurious mane.

"Oh, Captain!" he muttered, putting his face close to the animal's cheek. "You know what it is to fight for yourself! You know — but where you found love and help when you lost that fight, I'd find — just blackness — without even a candle —"

The stallion moved closer, shoving with his head until he forced VB out of the corral. Then with his teasing lips he sought the bridle.

"You seem to understand!" the man cried, his tired eyes lighting. "You seem to know what I need!"

Five minutes later he was rushing through the early morning air up the gulch, the Captain bearing him along with that free, firm, faultless stride that had swept him over those mountains for so many long, unmolested years.

Throughout the forenoon they rode hard. VB looked for the mare and colt, but the search did not command much of his attention.

"Why can't I turn all this longing into something useful?" he asked the horse. "Your lust for freedom has come to this end; why can't my impulses to be a wild beast be driven into another path?"

And the Captain made answer by bending his superb head and lipping VB's chap-clad knee.

The quest was fruitless, and an hour before noon VB turned back toward the ranch, making a short cut across the hills. In one of the gulches the Captain nickered softly and increased his trotting. VB let him go, unconscious of his brisker movement, for the calling in his throat had risen to a clamor. The horse stopped and lowered his head, drinking from a hole into which crystal water seeped.

The man dropped off and flopped on his stomach, thrusting his face into the pool close to the nose of the greedily drinking stallion. He took the water in great gulps. It was cold, as cold as spring water can be, yet it was as nothing against the fire within him.

The Captain, raising his head quickly, caught his breath with a grunt, dragging the air deep into his great lungs and exhaling slowly, loudly, as he gazed off down the gulch; then he chewed briskly on the bit and thrust his nose again into the spring.

VB's arm stole up and dropped over the horse's head.

"Oh, boy, you know what one kind of thirst is," he said in a whisper. "But there's another kind that this stuff won't quench! The thirst that comes from being in blackness —"

They went on, dropped off a point, and made for the flat little buildings of the ranch. As he approached, VB saw three saddled horses standing before the house, none of which was Jed's property. Nothing strange in that, however, for one man's home is another's shelter in that country, whether the owner be on the ground or not, and to VB the thought of visitors brought relief. Contact with others might joggle him from his mood.

He left the Captain, saddled, at the corral gate, bridle reins down, and he knew that the horse would not budge so much as a step until told to do so. Then he swung over toward the house, heels scuffing the hard dirt, spurs jingling. At the threshold he walked squarely into the man Rhues.

The recognition was a distinct shock. He stepped backward a pace — recoiled rather, for the movement was as from a thing he detested. Into his mind crowded every detail of his former encounters with this fellow; in the Anchor bunk house and across the road from the saloon in Ranger. They came back vividly — the expression of faces, lights and shadows, even odors, and the calling in him for the help that throttles became agonizing.

Rhues misconstrued his emotion. His judgment was warped by the spirit of the bully, and he thought this man feared him. He remembered that defiant interchange of questions, and the laugh that went to VB on their first meeting. He nursed the rankling memory. He had told it about that Avery's tenderfoot was afraid to take a drink — speaking greater truth than he was aware — but his motive had been to discredit VB in the eyes of the countrymen, for he belonged to that ilk who see in debauchery the mark of manhood.

Coming now upon the man he had chosen to persecute, and reading fear in VB's eyes, Rhues was made crudely happy.

"You don't appear to be overglad to see us," he drawled.

VB glanced into the room. A Mexican sat on the table, smoking and swinging his legs; a white man he remembered having seen in Ranger stood behind Rhues. Jed was nowhere about. He looked back at the snaky leer in those half-opened green eyes, and a rage went boiling into his brain. The unmistakable challenge which came from this bully was of the sort that strips from men civilization's veneer.

"You've gessed it," he said calmly. "I don't know why I should be glad to see you. These others" — he motioned — "are strangers to me."

Then he stepped past Rhues into the room.

The man grinned at him as he tossed his hat to a chair and unbuckled the leather cuffs.

"But that makes no difference," he went on. "Jed isn't here. It's meal time, and if you men want to eat I'll build a big enough dinner."

Rhues laughed, and the mockery in his tone was of the kind that makes the biggest of men forget they can be above insult.

"We did n't come here to eat," he said. "We come up to see a horse we heerd about—th' Captain. We heerd Jed caught him."

VB started. The thought of Rhues inspecting the stallion, commenting on him, admiring him, was as repulsive to Young VB as would be the thought to a lover of a vile human commenting vulgarly on the sacred body of the woman of women.

The Mexican strolled out of the house as VB, turning to the stove, tried to ignore the explanation of their presence. He walked on toward the ponies. A dozen steps from the house he stopped, and called:

"*Por Dios, hombre!*"

Rhues and the other followed him, and VB saw them stand together, staring in amazement at the Captain. Then they moved toward the great horse, talking to one another and laughing.

VB followed, with a feeling of indignation. The trio advanced, quickening their pace.

"Hold on!" he cried in sudden alarm. "Don't go too near; he's dangerous!"

Already the Captain had flattened his ears, and as VB ran out he could see the nose wrinkling, the lips drawing back.

"What's got into you?" demanded Rhues, turning, while the Mexican laughed jeeringly. "I guess if you can ride him a *man* can git up clost without gittin' chawed up! Remember, young kid, we've been workin' with hosses sence you was suckin' yer thumb."

The others laughed again, but VB gave no heed. He was seeing red again; reason had gone — either reason or the coating of conventions.

"Well, if you won't stand away from him because of danger, you'll do it because I say so!" he muttered.

"O-ho, an' that's it!" laughed Rhues, walking on.

VB passed him and approached the Captain and took his bridle.

"Be still, boy," he murmured. "Stand where you are."

He stroked the nose, and the wrinkles left it.

Rhues laughed again harshly.

"Well, that's a fine kind o' buggy horse!" he jeered. "Let a tenderfoot come up an' steal all th' man-eatin' fire outen him!"

He laughed again and the others joined. The Mexican said something in Spanish.

"Yah," assented Rhues. "I thought we was comin' to see a *hoss* — th' kind o' nag this feller pertended to be. But now — look at him! He's just a low-down ——"

VB sprang toward him.

"You —" he breathed, "you — you hound! Why, you aren't fit to come into sight of this horse. You — you apologize to that horse!" he demanded, and even through his molten rage the words sounded unutterably silly.

Yet he went on, fists clenched, carried beyond reason or balance by the instinctive hate for this man and love for the black animal behind him.

Rhues laughed again.

"Who says so, besides you, you ——. Why, you ain't no more man'n that hoss is hoss!"

He saw then that he had reckoned poorly. The greenhorn, the boy who cowered at the thought of a man's dissipation, had disappeared, and in his stead stood a quivering young animal, poising for a pounce.

Being a bully, Rhues was a coward. So when VB sprang, and he knew conflict was unavoidable, his right hand whipped back. The fingers closed on the handle of his automatic as VB made the first step. They made their hold secure as the Easterner's arm drew back. They yanked at the gun as that fist shot out.

It was a good blow, a clean blow, a full blow right on the point of the chin, and, quickly as it had been delivered, the right was back in an instinctive guard and the left had rapped out hard on the snarling mouth. Rhues went backward and down, unbalanced by the first shock, crushed by the second; and the third, a repeated jab of the left, caught him behind the ear and stretched him helpless in the dust.

His fingers relaxed their hold on the gun that he had not been quick enough to use, so lightning-like was the attack from this individual he had dubbed a "kid." VB stepped over the prostrate form, put his toe under the revolver, and flipped it a dozen yards away.

Then Jed Avery pulled up his horse in a shower of dust, and VB, his rage choking down words, turned to lead the Captain into the corral. The animal nosed him fiercely and pulled back to look at Rhues, who, under the crude ministrations of his two companions, had taken on a semblance of life.

A moment later VB returned from the inclosure, bearing his riding equipment. He said to Jed: "This man insulted the Captain. I had to whip him." Then he walked to the wagon shed, dropped his saddle in its shelter, and came back.

Rhues sat up and, as VB approached, got to his feet. He lurched forward as if to rush his enemy, but the Mexican caught him and held him back.

VB stood, hands on hips, and glared at him. He said: "No, I wouldn't come again if I were you. I don't want to have to smash you again. I'd enjoy it in a way, but when a man is knocked out he's whipped — in my country — judged by the standards we set there.

"You're a coward, Rhues — a dirty, sneaking, low-down coward! Every gun-man is a coward. It's no way to settle disputes — gun fighting."

He glared at the fellow before him, who swore under his breath but who could not summon the courage to strike.

"You're a coward, and I hope I've impressed that on you," VB went on, "and you'll take a coward's advantage. Hereafter I'm going to carry a gun. You won't fight in my way because you're not a man, so I'll have to be prepared for you in your way. I just want to let you know that I understand your breed! That's all.

"Don't start anything, because I'll fight in two ways hereafter — in my way and in yours. And that goes for you other two. If you run with this — this *thing*, it marks you. I know what would have happened if Jed had n't come up. You'd have killed me! That's the sort you are. Remember — all three of you — I'm not afraid, but it's a case of fighting fire with fire. I'll be ready."

Rhues stood, as though waiting for more.

When VB did not go on he said, just above a whisper: "I'll get you — yet!"

And VB answered, "Then I guess we all understand one another."

When the three had ridden away Jed shoved his Colt tight into its holster again and looked at the young chap with foreboding.

"There'll be trouble, VB; they're bad," he said. "He's a coward. The story'll go round an' he'll try to get you harder 'n ever. If he don't, those others will — will try, I mean. Matson and Julio are every bit as bad as Rhues, but they ain't quite got his fool nerve.

"They're a thievin' bunch, though it ain't never been proved. Nobody trusts 'em; most men let 'em alone an' wait fer 'em to show their hand. They've been cute; they've been suspected, but they ain't never got out on a limb.

They've got a lot to cover up, no doubt. But they've got a grudge now. An' when cowards carry grudges — look out!"

"If a man like Rhues were all I had to fear, I should never worry," VB muttered, weak again after the excitement. "He's bad — but there are worse things — that you can't have the satisfaction of knocking down."

And his conspiring nostrils smelled whisky in that untainted air.

CHAPTER XIV

The Schoolhouse Dance

YOUNG VB held a twofold interest for the men of Clear River. First, the story of his fight with the Captain spread over the land, percolating to the farthest camps. Men laughed at first. The absurdity of it! Then, their surprise giving way to their appreciation of his attainment, their commendation for the young Easterner soared to superlatively profane heights.

When he met those who had been strangers before it was to be scrutinized and questioned and frankly, honestly admired.

Now came another reason for discussing him about bunk-house stoves. He had thrashed Rhues! Great as had been the credit accorded VB for the capture of the stallion, just so great was men's delight caused by the outcome of that other encounter.

They remembered, then, how Rhues had told of the greenhorn who was afraid to take a drink; how he had made it a purpose to spread stories of ridicule, doing his best to pervert the community's natural desire to let the affairs of others alone. And this recollection of Rhues's bullying was an added reason for their saying: "Good! I'm glad to hear it. Too bad th' kid did n't beat him to death!"

Though his meetings with other men were few and scattered, VB was coming to be liked. It mattered little to others why he was in the country, from where he came, or who he had been. He had accomplished two worthy things among them, and respect was accorded him across vast distances. Dozens of these men had seen him only once, and scores never, yet they reckoned him of their number — a man to be taken seriously, worthy of their kindly attention, of their interest, and of their respect.

Bob Thorpe helped to establish VB in the mountains. He thought much about his interview with the young chap, and told to a half-dozen men the story which, coming from him, had weight.

His daughter did not abandon her idea of owning the Captain. Bob told her repeatedly that it was useless to argue with a man who spoke as did Jed's rider; but the girl chose to disagree with him.

"I think that if you'd flatter him enough — if we both would — that he would listen. Don't you?" she asked.

Bob Thorpe shook his head.

"No," he answered. "You can't convince me of that. You don't know men, and I do. I've seen one or two like him before — who love a thing of that sort above money; and, I've found you can't do a thing with 'em — ding 'em!"

The girl cried: "Why, don't feel that way

about it! I think it's perfectly fine — to love an animal so much that money won't buy him!"

"Sure it is," answered her father. "That's what makes me out of patience with them. They're — they're better men than most of us, and — well, they make a fellow feel rather small at times."

Then he went away, and Gail puzzled over his concluding remark.

A week to a day after her first visit she drove again to Jed's ranch.

"I came over to see the Captain," she told the old man gayly.

"Well, th' Captain ain't here now," he answered, beaming on her; "but VB'll be back with him before noon."

She looked for what seemed to be an unnecessarily long time at her watch, and then asked:

"Is that his name?"

"What — th' Captain?"

"No — VB."

Jed laughed silently at her.

"Yep — to be sure an' that's his name — all th' name he's got."

"Well, I wish Mr. VB would hurry back with the Captain," she said.

But that easy flush was again in her cheeks, and the turn she gave the conversation was, as they say in certain circles, poor footwork.

Within an hour the Captain bore his rider home. Gail stayed for dinner and ate with the two men.

It was a strange meal for VB. Not in months had he eaten at the same table with a woman; not in years had he broken bread with a woman such as this, and realization of the fact carried him back beyond those darkest days. He remembered suddenly and quite irrelevantly that he once had wondered if this daughter of Bob Thorpe's was to be a connecting link with the old life. That had been when he first learned that the big cattleman had a daughter, and that she was living in his East. Now as he sat before neglected food and watched and listened, feasting his starved spirit on her, noting her genuine vivacity, her enthusiasm, the quick come and go of color in her fine skin, he knew that she was a link, but not with the past that he had feared. She took him back beyond that, into his earlier boyhood, that period of adolescence when, to a clean-minded boy, all things are good and unstained. She was attractive in all the ways that women can be attractive, and at the same time she was more than a desirable individual; she seemed to stand for classes, for modes of living and thinking, that Young VB had put behind him — put behind first by his wasting, now by distance. But as the meal progressed a fresh wonder crept up in his mind. Was all that really so very far away? Was not the distance just that between them and the big ranch house under the cottonwoods beyond the hills? And was the result of his wasting quite irreparable?

Was he not rebuilding what he had torn down?

He felt himself thrilling and longing suddenly for fresher, newer experiences as the talk ran on between the others. The conversation was wholly of the country, and VB was surprised to discover that this girl could talk intelligently and argue effectively with Jed over local stock conditions when she looked for all the world like any of the hundreds he could pick out on Fifth Avenue at five o'clock of any fine afternoon. He corrected himself hastily. She was *not* like those others, either. She possessed all their physical endowments, all and more, for her eye was clearer, her carriage better, she was possessed of a color that was no sham; and a finer body. Put her beside them in their own environment, and they would seem stale by comparison; bring those others here, and their bald artificiality would be pathetic. The boy wanted her to know those things, yet thought of telling her never came to his consciousness. Subjectively he was humble before her.

The interest between the two young people was not centered completely in VB. Each time he lowered his gaze to his plate he was conscious of those frank, intelligent blue eyes on him, studying, prying, wondering, a laugh ever deep within them. Now and then the girl addressed a remark to him, but for the most part she spoke directly to Jed; however, she was studying the boy every instant, quietly, carefully, missing no detail, and by the time the meal neared its end the laughter had left her eyes and they betrayed a frank curiosity.

When the meal was finished the girl asked VB to take her to the corral. She made the request lightly, but it smote something in the man a teriffic blow, stirring old memories, fresh desires, and he was strangely glad that he could do something for her. As they walked from the cabin to the inclosure he was flushed, embarrassed, awkward. He could not talk to her, could scarcely keep his body from swinging from side to side with schoolboy shyness.

The stallion did not fidget at sight of the girl as he had done on the approach of other strangers. He snorted and backed away, keeping his eyes on her and his ears up with curiosity, coming to a halt against the far side of the corral and switching his fine tail down over the shapely hocks as though to make these people understand that in spite of his seeming harmlessness he might yet show the viciousness that lurked down in his big heart.

"I think he'll come to like you," said VB, looking from his horse to the girl. "I don't see how he could help it — to like women, understand," he added hastily when she turned a wide-eyed gaze on him. "He does n't like strange men, but see — he's interested in you; and it's curiosity, not anger. I — I don't blame him — for being interested," he ventured, and hated himself for the flush that swept up from his neck.

They both laughed, and Gail said: "So this country hasn't taken the flattery out of you?"

"Why, it's been years — years since I said a thing like that to a girl of your sort," VB answered soberly.

An awkward pause followed.

"Dare I touch him?" the girl finally asked.

"No, I wouldn't to-day," VB advised. "Just let him look at you now. Some other time we'll see if — That is, if you'll ever come to see us — to see the Captain again."

"I should like to come to see the Captain very much, and as often as is proper," she said with mocking demureness.

And she did come again; and again and yet again. Always she took pains to begin with inquiries about the horse. When she did this in Jed Avery's presence it was with a peculiar avoidance of his gaze, that might have been from embarrassment; when she asked Young VB those questions it was with a queer little teasing smile. A half-dozen times she found the boy alone at the ranch, and the realization that on such occasions she stayed longer than she did when Jed was about gave him a new thrill of delight.

At first there was an awkward reserve between them, but after the earlier visits this broke down and their talk became interspersed with personal references, with small, inconsequential confidences that, intrinsically worthless, meant much to them. Yet there was never a word of the life both had lived far over the other side of those snowcaps to the eastward. Somehow the girl felt intuitively that it had not all been pleasant for the man there, and VB maintained a stubborn reticence. He could have told her much of her own life back in the East, of the things she liked, of the events and conditions that were irksome, because he knew the environment in which she had lived and he felt that he knew the girl herself. He would not touch that topic, however, for it would lead straight to *his* life; and all that he wanted for his thoughts now were Jed and the hills and the Captain and — this girl. They composed a comfortable world of which he wanted to be a part.

Gail found herself feeling strangely at home with this young fellow. She experienced a mingled feeling compounded of her friendship for the finished youths she had known during school days and that which she felt for the men of her mountains, who were, she knew, as rugged, as genuine, as the hills themselves. To her Young VB rang true from the ground up, and he bore the finish that can come only from contact with many men. That is a rare combination.

It came about that after a time the Captain let Gail touch him, allowed her to walk about him and caress his sleek body. Always, when she was near, he stood as at attention, dignified and self-conscious, and from time to time his eyes would seek the face of his master, as though for reassurance. Once after the girl had gone VB took the Captain's face between his hands and, looking into the big black eyes, muttered almost fiercely:

"She's as much of the real stuff as you are, old boy! Do you think, Captain, that I can ever match up with you two?"

Before a month had gone by the girl could lead the Captain about, could play with him almost as familiarly as VB did; but always the horse submitted as if uninterested, went through this formality of making friends as though it were a duty that bored him.

Once Dick Worth, the deputy from Sand Creek, and his wife rode up the gulch to see the black stallion. While the Captain would not allow the man near him, he suffered the woman to tweak his nose and slap his cheeks and pull his ears; then it was that Jed and VB knew that the animal understood the difference between sexes and that the chivalry which so became him had been cultivated by his intimacy with Gail Thorpe.

After that, of course, there was no plausible excuse for Gail's repeated visits. However, she continued coming. VB was always reserved up to a certain point before her, never yielding beyond it in spite of the strength of the subtle tactics she employed to draw him out. A sense of uncertainty of himself held him aloof. Within him was a traditional respect for women. He idealized them, and then set for men a standard which they must attain before meeting women as equals. But this girl, while satisfying his ideal, would not remain aloof. She forced herself into VB's presence, forced herself, and yet with a delicacy that could not be misunderstood. She came regularly, her visits lengthened, and one sunny afternoon as they stood watching the Captain roll she looked up sharply at the man beside her.

"Why do you keep me at this?"

"This? What? I don't get your meaning."

"At coming over here? Why don't you come to see me? I— Of course, I have n't any fine horse to show you, but—"

Her voice trailed off, with a hint of wounded pride in the tone. The man faced her, stunning surprise in his face.

"You — you don't think I fail to value this friendship of ours?" he demanded, rallying. "You— Why, what can I say to you? It has meant so much to me — just seeing you; it's been one of the finest things of this fine country. But I thought — I thought it was because of this,"— with a gesture toward the Captain, who stood shaking the dust from his hair with mighty effort. "I thought all along you were interested in the horse; not that you cared about knowing me —"

"Did you really think that?" she broke in.

VB flushed, then laughed, with an abrupt change of mood.

"Well, it *began* that way," he pleaded weakly.

"And you'd let it end that way."

"Oh, no; you don't understand, Miss Thorpe," serious again. "I — I can't explain, and you don't understand now. But I've felt somehow as though it would be presuming too much if I came to see you."

She looked at him calculatingly a long moment as he twirled his hat and kicked at a pebble with his boot.

"I think it would be presuming too much if you let me do all the traveling, since you admit that a friendship does exist," she said lightly.

"Then the only gallant thing for me to do is to call on you."

"I think so. I'm glad you recognize the fact."

"When shall it be?"

"Any time. If I'm not home, stay until I get back. Daddy likes you. You'll love my mother."

The vague "any time" occurred three days later. Young VB made a special trip over the hills to the S Bar S. The girl was stretched in a hammock, reading, when he rode up, and at the sound of his horse she scrambled to her feet, flushed, and evidently disconcerted.

"I'd given you up!" she cried.

"In three days?" taking the hand she offered.

"Well — most boys in the East would have come the next morning — if they were really interested."

"This is Colorado," he reminded her.

He sat crosslegged on the ground at her feet,

and they talked of the book she had been reading. It was a novel of music and a musician and a rare achievement, she said. He questioned her about the story, and their talk drifted to music, on which they both could converse well.

"You don't know what it means—to sit here and talk of these things with you," he said hungrily.

"Well, I should like to know," she said, leaning forward over her knees.

For two long hours they talked as they never had talked before; of personal tastes, of kindred enthusiasms, of books and plays and music and people. They went into the ranch house, and Gail played for him — on the only grand piano in that section of the state. They came out, and she saddled her pony to ride part way back through the hills with him.

"*Adios*, my friend," she called after him, as he swung away from her.

"It's your turn to call now," he shouted back to her, and when the ridge took him from sight he leaned low to the Captain's ear and repeated gently, — "my friend!"

So the barrier of reserve was broken. VB did not dare think into the future in any connection — least of all in relation to this new and growing friendship; yet he wanted to make their understanding more complete though he would scarcely admit that fact even to himself.

A week had not passed when Gail Thorpe drove the automobile up to the VB gate.

THE SCHOOLHOUSE DANCE 175

"I did n't come to see the Captain this time," she announced to them both. "I came to pay a party call to Mr. VB, and to include Mr. Avery. Because when a girl out here receives a visit from a man it's of party proportions!"

As she was leaving, she asked, "Why don't you come down to the dance Friday night?"

"A big event?"

"Surely!" She laughed merrily. "It's the first one since spring, and everybody'll be there. Mr. Avery will surely come. Won't you, too, Mr. VB?"

He evaded her, but when she had turned the automobile about and sped down the road, homeward bound, he let down the bars for youth's romanticism and knew that he would dance with her if it meant walking every one of the twenty-two miles to the schoolhouse.

For the first time in years VB felt a thrill at the anticipation of a social function, and with it a guilty little thought kept buzzing in the depths of his mind. The thought was: Is her hair as fragrant as it is glorious in color and texture?

Jed and VB made the ride after supper, over frozen paths, for autumn had aged and the tang of winter was in the air. Miles away they could see the glow of the bonfire that had been built before the little stone schoolhouse; and VB was not sorry that Jed wanted to ride the last stages of the trip at a faster pace.

Clear River had turned out, to the last man and woman — and to the last child, too! The schoolhouse was no longer a seat of learning; it was a festal bower. The desks had been taken up and placed along the four walls, seats outward, tops forming a ledge against the calcimined stones, making a splendid place for those youngest children who had turned out! Yes, a dozen babies slumbered there in the confusion, wrapped in many thicknesses of blankets.

Three lamps with polished reflectors were placed on window ledges, and the yellow glare filled the room with just sufficient brilliance to soften lines in faces and wrinkles in gowns that clung to bodies in unexpected places. The fourth window ledge was reserved for the music — a phonograph with a morning-glory horn, a green morning-glory horn that would have baffled a botanist. The stove blushed as if for its plainness in the center of the room, and about it, with a great scraping of feet and profound efforts to be always gentlemanly and at ease, circled the men, guiding their partners.

VB stood in the doorway and watched. He coughed slightly from the dust that rose and mantled everything with a dulling blanket — everything, I said, but the eyes must be excepted. They flashed with as warm a brilliance as they ever do where there is music and dancing and laughter.

The music stopped. Women scurried to their

THE SCHOOLHOUSE DANCE

seats; some lifted the edges of blankets and peered with concerned eyes at the little sleepers lying there, then whirled about and opened their arms to some new gallant; for so brief was the interval between dances.

"Well, are you never going to see me?"

VB started at the sound of Gail's voice so close to him. He bowed and smiled at her.

"I was interested," he said in excuse. "Getting my bearings."

She did not reply, but the expectancy in her face forced his invitation, and they joined the swirl about the stove.

"I can't dance in these riding boots," he confided with an embarrassed laugh. "Never thought about it until now."

"Oh, yes, you can! You dance much better than most men. Don't stop, please!"

He knew that no woman who danced with Gail's lightness could find pleasure in the stumbling, stilted accompaniment of his handicapped feet; and the conviction sent a fresh thrill through him. He was glad she wanted him to keep on! She had played upon the man down in him and touched upon vanity, one of those weak spots in us. She wanted him near. His arm, spite of his caution, tightened a trifle and he suddenly knew that her hair *was* as fragrant as it should be — a heavy, rich odor that went well with its other wealth! For an instant he was a bit giddy, but as the music came to a stop he recovered himself and walked silently beside Gail to a seat.

After that he danced with the wife of a cattleman, and answered absently her stammered advances at communication while he watched the floating figure of Gail Thorpe as it followed the bungling lead of her father's foreman.

The end of the intermission found him with her again. As they whirled away his movements became a little quicker, his tongue a little looser. It had been a long time since he had felt so gay.

He learned of the other women, Gail telling him about them as they danced, and through the thrill that her warm breath aroused he found himself delighting in the individuality of her expression, the stamping of a characteristic in his mind by a queer little word or twisted phrase. He discovered, too, that she possessed a penetrating insight into the latent realities of life. The red-handed, blunt, strong women about him, who could ride with their husbands and brothers, who could face hardships, who knew grim elementals, became new beings under the interpretation of this sunny-haired girl; took on a charm tinged with pathos that brought up within VB a sympathy that those struggles in himself had all but buried. And the knowledge that Gail appreciated those raw realities made him look down at her lingeringly, a trifle wonderingly.

She was of that other life — the life of refinements — in so many ways, yet she had escaped its host of artificialities. She had lifted herself above the people among whom she was reared; but her touch, her sympathies, her warm humanness remained unalloyed! She was real.

And then, when he was immersed in this appreciation of her, she turned the talk suddenly to him. He was but slightly responsive. He put her off, evaded, but he laughed; his cold reluctance to let her know him had ceased to be so stern, and her determination to get behind his silence rose.

As they stood in the doorway in a midst of repartee she burst on him:

"Mr. VB, why do you go about with that awful name? It's almost as bad as being branded."

He sobered so quickly that it frightened her.

"Maybe I am branded," he said slowly, and her agile understanding caught the significance of his tone. "Perhaps I'm branded and can't use another. Who knows?"

He smiled at her, but from sobered eyes. Confused by his evident seriousness, she made one more attempt, and laughed: "Well, if you won't tell me who you are, won't you please tell me what you are?"

The door swung open then, and on the heels of her question came voices from without. One voice rose high above the rest, and they heard: "Aw, come on; le's have jus' one more little drag at th' bottle!"

VB looked at Gail a bit wildly.

Those words meant that out there whisky was

waiting for him, and at its mention that searing thing sprang alive in his throat!

"What am I?" he repeated dully, trying to rally himself. "What am I?" Unknowingly his fingers gripped her arm. "Who knows? I don't!"

And he flung out of the place, wanting but one thing — to be with the Captain, to feel the stallion's nose in his arms, to stand close to the body which housed a spirit that knew no defeat.

As he strode past the bonfire a man's face leered at him from the far side. The man was Rhues.

CHAPTER XV

MURDER

THE incident at the schoolhouse was not overlooked. Gail Thorpe was not the only one who heard and saw and understood; others connected the mention of drink with VB's sudden departure. The comment went around in whispers at the dance, to augment and amplify those other stories which had arisen back in the Anchor bunk house and which had been told by Rhues of the meeting in Ranger.

"Young VB *is* afraid to take a drink," declared a youth to a group about the fire where they discussed the incident.

He laughed lightly and Dick Worth looked sharply at the boy.

"Mebby he is," he commented, reprimand in his tone, "an' mebby it'd be a good thing for some o' you kids if you was afraid. Don't laugh at him! We know he's pretty much man — 'cause he's done real things since comin' in here a rank greenhorn. Don't laugh! You ought to help, instead o' that."

And the young fellow, taking the rebuke, admitted: "I guess you're right. Maybe the booze has put a crimp in him."

So VB gave the community one more cause for

watching him. Quick to perceive, ever taking into consideration his achievements which spoke of will and courage, Clear River gave him silent sympathy, and promptly put the matter out of open discussion. It was no business of theirs so long as VB kept it to himself. Yet they watched, knowing a fight was being waged and guessing at the outcome, the older and wiser ones hoping while they guessed.

When Bob Thorpe announced to his daughter that he was going to Jed Avery's ranch and would like to have her drive him over through the first feathery dusting of snow, a strain of unpleasant thinking which had endured for three days was broken for the girl. In fact, her relief was so evident that the cattleman stared hard at his daughter.

"You're mighty enthusiastic about that place, seems to me," he remarked.

"Why shouldn't I be?" she asked. "There's where they keep the finest horse in this country!"

"Is that all?" he asked, a bit grimly.

She looked at him and laughed. Then, coming close, she patted one of the weathered cheeks.

"He's awfully nice, daddy — and so mysterious!"

The giggle she forced somehow reassured him. He did not know it was forced.

They arrived at Jed's ranch as Kelly, the horse buyer, was preparing to depart after long weeks in the country. His bunch was in the lower pasture and two saddle horses waited at the gate.

Thorpe and his daughter found Jed, VB, and Kelly in the cabin. The horse buyer was just putting bills back into his money belt, and Jed still fingered the roll that he had taken for his horses.

"Aren't you afraid to pack all that around, Kelly?" Thorpe asked.

"No — nobody holds people up any more," he laughed. "There's only an even six hundred there, anyhow — and a fifty-dollar bill issued by the Confederate States of America, which I carry for luck. My father was a raider with Morgan," he explained, "and I was fifteen years old before I knew 'damn Yank' was two words!"

VB was preparing to go with the buyer, to ride the first two days at least to help him handle the bunch. They expected to make it well out of Ranger the second day, and after that Kelly would pick up another helper.

Gail followed VB when he went outside.

"I'm going away, too," she said.

"So?"

"Yes; mother and I will leave for California day after to-morrow, for the winter."

"That will be fine!"

"Will I be missed?"

He shrank from this personal talk. He remembered painfully their last meeting. He was acutely conscious of how it had ended, and knew that the incident of his abrupt departure must have set her wondering.

"Yes," he answered, meeting her answer truthfully, "I shall miss you. I like you."

Such a thing from him was indeed a jolt, and Gail stooped to pick up a wisp of hay to cover her confusion.

"But I'm sorry," he said, "I must be going."

She looked up in surprise. The horse buyer still talked and the discussion bade fair to go on for a long time.

"You're not starting?" she asked.

"Oh, no. Not for half an hour, anyhow. But you see, the Captain found a pup-hole yesterday and wrenched his leg a little. Not much, but I don't want him to work when anything's wrong. So I'm leaving him behind and I must look after him. Will you excuse me? Good-by!"

She was so slow in extending her hand that he was forced to reach down for it. It was limp within his, and she merely mumbled a response to his hasty farewell.

Gail watched him swing off toward the corral, saw him enter through the gate and put his face against the stallion's neck. She strolled toward the car, feet heavy.

"He wouldn't even ask me to go — go with him. He cares more about — that horse — than —"

She clenched her fists and whispered: "I hate you! I hate you!" Then mounting to the seat and tucking the robe about her ankles, she blew her nose, wiped her eyes, and in a voice strained high said: "No, I don't, either."

VB and Kelly took their bunch down the gulch at a spanking trot. Most of the stock was fairly gentle and they had little difficulty. They planned to stop at a deserted cabin a few miles north of Ranger where a passable remnant of fenced pasture still remained. They reached the place at dark and made a hasty meal, after which VB rolled in, but his companion roped a fresh horse and made on to Ranger for a few hours' diversion.

It was nearly dawn when Kelly returned with a droll account of the night's poker, and although VB was for going on early, wanting to be rid of the task, the other insisted on sleeping.

"I don't want to get too far, anyhow," he said. "Those waddies like to rimmed me last night. Got all I had except what's in old Betsy, the belt. I'm goin' back to-night and get their scalp!"

It was noon before they reached Ranger and swung to the east.

"Oh, I'll be back to-night and get you fellows!" Kelly called to a man who waved to him from the saloon.

VB held his gaze in the opposite direction. He knew that even the sight of the place might raise the devil in him again.

A man emerged from one of the three isolated shacks down on the river bank. It was Rhues.

The two rode slowly, for the buyer was in no mood for fast travel, and for a long time Rhues stood there following them with his eyes.

At dusk the horsemen turned the bunch into a corral and prepared to spend the night with beds spread in the ruin of a cabin near the inclosure. Before the bed-horses had been relieved of their burdens a cowboy rode along who was known to Kelly, and arrangements were made for him to take VB's place on the morrow.

"Well, then, all you want me to do is to stay here to-night to see that things don't go wrong. Is that it?" VB asked.

"Yep— Oh, I don't know," with a yawn. "I guess I won't sit in that game to-night. I'll get some sleep. Mebby if I did go back I'd only have to dig up part of my bank here." He patted his waist. "You can go on home if you want to."

VB was glad to be released, for he could easily reach the ranch that night. He left Kelly talking with the cowboy, making their plans for the next day, and struck across the country for Jed's ranch.

Left alone, the horse buyer munched a cold meal. Then, shivering, he crept into his thick bed and slept. An hour passed — two — three.

A horse dropped slowly off a point near the corral. A moment later two more followed. One rider dismounted and walked away after a low, hoarse whisper; another pushed his horse into the highway and stood still, listening; the third held the pony that had been left riderless.

A figure, worming its way close to the ground, crawled up on the sleeping horse buyer. It moved silently, a yard at a time; then stopped, raised its head as though to listen; on again, ominously, so much a part of the earth it covered that it might have been just the ridge raised by a giant mole burrowing along under the surface. It approached to within three yards of the sleeping man; to within six feet; three; two.

Then it rose to its knees slowly, cautiously, silently, and put out a hand gently, lightly feeling the outlines of the blankets. A shoot of orange scorched the darkness — and another, so close together that the flame was almost continuous. The blankets heaved, trembled, settled.

The man on his knees hovered a long moment, revolver ready, listening intently. Not a sound — even the horses seemed to be straining their ears for another break in the night.

The man reached out a hand and drew the blankets away from the figure beneath, thrusting his face close. The starlight filtered in and he drew a long, quivering breath — not in hate or horror, but in surprise. He got to his feet and listened again. Then he moved into the open, over the way he had come. After a dozen quick, stealthy paces he stopped and turned back. He unbuttoned the jumper about the figure under the blankets, unbuttoned the shirt, felt quickly about the waist, fumbled a moment, and jerked out a long, limp object. Again he strode catlike into the open, and as he went he tucked the money belt into his shirt-front.

VB rode straight to the ranch. He made a quick ride and arrived before ten.

"Mighty glad Kelly got that man," he told Jed. "I'm like a fish out of water away from the Captain."

At dusk the next day a horseman rode up the gulch to Jed's outfit. The old man stood in the doorway, watching him approach.

"Hello, Dick!" he called, recognizing the deputy from Sand Creek.

"How's things, Jed?"

"Better'n fine."

Worth left his horse and entered the cabin.

"VB around?" he asked.

"Uh-huh; out in th' corral foolin' with th' Captain."

Dick dropped to a chair and pushed his hat back. He looked on the other a moment, then asked: "What time did VB get home last night?"

Jed showed evident surprise, but answered: "Between half-past nine an' ten."

"Notice his horse?"

"Saw him this mornin'. Why?"

"Was it a hard ride th' boy made?"

"No — sure not. I rode th' pony down to th' lower pasture myself this afternoon."

MURDER

Worth drew a deep breath and smiled as though relieved.

"Bein' 'n officer is mighty onpleasant sometimes," he confessed. "I knew it was n't no use to ask them questions, but I had to do it — 'cause I'm a deputy." With mouth set, Jed waited for the explanation he knew must come.

"Kelly was killed while he slept last night."

Horror was the first natural impulse for a man to experience on the knowledge of such a tragedy, but horror did not come to Jed Avery then or for many minutes. He put out a hand slowly and felt for the table as though dizzy.

Then, in a half tone, "You don't mean you suspected VB? Dick — *Dick!*"

The sheriff's face became troubled.

"Jed, did n't I tell you I knew it was n't no use to ask them questions?" he said reassuringly. "I'd 'a' gambled my outfit on th' boy, 'cause I know what he is. When you tell me he got here by ten an' it was n't a hard ride, I know they's no use even thinkin' about it. But th' fact is —

"You see, Jed, everybody in th' country has got to know what's up with VB. They know he's fightin' back th' booze! That gang o' skunks down at Ranger — Rhues an' his outfit — started out to rub it into VB, but everybody knew they was tellin' lies. An' everybody's thought lots of him fer th' fight he's made."

He got to his feet and walked slowly about the room.

"But th' truth is, Jed — an' you know it — when a man's been hittin' th' booze, an' we ain't sure he's beat it out, we're always lookin' fer him to slip. Nobody down at Ranger has thought one word about VB in this, only that mebby he could tell who'd been round there.

"But, bein' 'n officer, I had th' sneakin', dirty idee I ought to ask them questions about VB. That's all there is to it, Jed. That's all! I'm deputy; VB's been a boozer.

"But I tell you, Jed Avery, it sure's a relief to know it's all right."

The warmth of sincerity was in his tone and his assurances had been of the best, but Jed slumped limply into a chair and rested his head on his hands.

"It's a rotten world, Dick — a rotten, rotten world!" he said. "I know you're all right; I know you mean what you say; but ain't it a shame that when a man's down our first thought is to kick him? Always expect him to fall again once he gets up! Ain't it rotten?"

And his love for Young VB, stirred anew by this sense of the injustice of things, welled into his throat, driving back more words.

Dick Worth was a man of golden integrity; Jed knew well that no suspicion would be cast on VB. But the knowledge that serious-minded, clear-thinking men like the deputy would always remember, in a time like this, that those who had once run wild might fall into the old ways at any hour, stung him like a lash.

MURDER

VB opened the door.

"Hello, Dick!" he greeted cheerily. "Want me?"

Worth laughed and Jed started.

"No; I come up to get a little help from you if I can, though."

"Help?"

"Kelly was shot dead in his bed last night."

For a moment VB stared at him.

"Who?"

"That's what we don't know. That's what I came up here for — to see if you could help us."

And Jed, face averted, drew a foot quickly across the boards of the floor.

"One of Hank Redden's boys was with him — th' one who took your place — until dark. Little after eight old Hank heard two shots, but did n't think nothin' of it. Kelly was shot twice. That must 'a' been th' time."

VB put down his hat, his eyes bright with excitement.

"He'd planned to go back to Ranger," he said. "But, after being up most of the night before, he was too tired. He told them at Ranger he'd be back. And if I'd been there they'd have got me," he ended.

"Unless they was lookin' for Kelly especial," said Dick. "They took his money belt."

"Mebby," muttered Jed,— "mebby they made a mistake."

CHAPTER XVI

THE CANDLE BURNS

TIME went on, and the country dropped back from the singing pitch of excitement to which the killing of the horse buyer raised it. Men agreed that some one of that country had fired the shots into that blanket, but it is not a safe thing to suspect too openly. Dick Worth worked continually, but his efforts were without result. A reward of two hundred and fifty dollars for the slayer, dead or alive, disclosed nothing.

After the evidence had been sifted, and each man had asked his quota of questions and passed judgment on the veracity of the myriad stories, Dick said to himself: "We'll settle down now and see who leaves the country."

Jed and VB went about the winter's work in a leisurely way. For days after the visit of Worth the old man was quieter than usual. The realization of how the world looked on this young fellow he had come to love had been driven in upon him. There could be no mistaking it; and as he reasoned the situation out, he recognized the attitude of men as the only logical thing to expect.

With his quietness came a new tenderness, a

THE CANDLE BURNS

deeper devotion. The two sat, one night, listening to the drawing of the stove and the whip of the wind as it sucked down the gulch. The candle burned steadily in its bottle. Jed watched it a long time, and, still gazing at the steady flame, he said, as though unconscious that thoughts found vocal expression: "Th' candle's burnin' bright, VB."

The other looked slowly around at it and smiled.

"Yes, Jed; it surely burns bright."

At the instant an unusually vicious gust of wind rattled the windows and a vagrant draft caught the flame of the taper, bending it low, dulling its orange.

"But yet sometimes," the younger man went on, "something comes along — something that makes it flicker — that takes some of the assurance from it."

Jed had started in his chair as the flame bowed before the draft.

"But it — You ain't been flickerin' lately, have you?" he asked, with a look in the old eyes that was beseeching.

Young VB rose and commenced to walk about thumbs hooked in his belt.

"I don't know, Jed," he said. "That's the whole of it: I don't know. Sometimes I'm glad I don't; but other times I wish — *wish* that whatever is coming would come. I seem to be gaining; I can think of drink now without going crazy. Now and then it gets hold of me; but moving around and getting busy stifles it. Still, I know it's there. That's what counts. I know I've had the habit, been down and out, and there's no telling which way it's going to turn. If I could ever be sure of myself; if I could ever come right up against it, where I needed a drink, where I wanted it — then, if I could refuse, I'd be sure."

He quickened his stride.

"Seems to me you're worryin' needless," Jed argued. "Don't you see, VB, this is th' worst night we've had; th' worst wind. An' yet it ain't blowed th' candle out! It bends low an' gets smoky, to be sure. But it always keeps on shinin'!"

"But when it bends low and gets smoky its resistance is lower," VB said. "It would n't take much at such a time to blow it out and let the darkness come in. You never can tell, Jed; you never can tell."

Ten minutes later he added: "Especially when you're afraid of yourself and dare n't hunt out a test."

Another time they talked of the man that he had been before he came to Colt. They were riding the hills, the Captain snuggling close to the pinto pony Jed rode. The sun poured its light down on the white land. Far away, over on the divide, they could see huge spirals of snow picked up by the wind and carried along countless miles, black's head and laughed happily into the soft neck.

"VB, you're a fool — a silly fool!" he whispered.

But if it was so, if being a fool made him that happy, he never wanted to regain mental balance.

It was a big evening for VB, perhaps the biggest of his life. Bob Thorpe and his family ate with the men. Democracy unalloyed was in his soul. He mingled with them not through condescension, but through desire, and his family maintained the same bearing. Not a cow-puncher in the country but who respected Mrs. Thorpe and Gail and would welcome an opportunity to fight for them.

The men had finished their meal before VB and Jed entered. Mrs. Thorpe made excuses and went out, leaving the four alone. While Jed talked to her father, Gail, elbows on the table, chatted with VB, and Young VB could only stare at his plate and snatch a glance at her occasionally and wonder why it was that she so disturbed him.

Later Bob took Jed into his office, and when Gail and VB were left alone the constraint between them became even more painful. Try as he would, the man could not bring his scattered wits together for coherent speech. Just being beside that girl after her long absence was intoxicating, benumbing his mind, stifling in him all thought and action, creating a thralldom which was at once agony and peace. An intuitive sensing of this helplessness had made him delay seeing her that evening; now that he was before her he never wanted to leave; he wanted only to sit and listen to her voice and watch the alert expressiveness of her face — a mute, humble worshiper.

And this attitude of his forced a reaction on the girl. At first she talked vivaciously, starting each new subject with an enthusiasm that seemed bound to draw him out, but when he remained dumb and helpless in spite of her best efforts to keep the conversation going, her flow of words lagged. Long, wordless intervals followed, and a flush came into the girl's cheeks, and she too found herself woefully self-conscious. She sought for the refuge of diversion.

"Since you won't talk to me, Mr. VB," she said with an embarrassed laugh, "you are going to force me to play for you."

"It isn't that I won't — I *can't*," he stammered. "And please play."

He sat back in his chair, relieved, and watched the fine sway of her body as she made the big, full-toned instrument give up its soul. Music, that — not the tunes that most girls of his acquaintance had played for him; a St. Saens arrangement, a MacDowell sketch, a bit of Nevin, running from one theme into another, easily, naturally, grace everywhere, from the phrasing to the movements of her firm little shoulders.

And VB found his self-possession returning, found that he was thinking evenly, sanely, under the quieting influence of this music.

Then Gail paused, sitting silent before the keyboard, as though to herald a coming climax. She leaned closer over the instrument and struck into the somber strains of a composition of such grim power and beauty that it seemed to create for itself an oddly receptive attitude in the man, sensitizing his emotional nature to a point where its finest shades were brought out in detail. It went on and on through its various phases to the end, and on the heavy final chord the girl's hands dropped into her lap. For a moment she sat still bent toward the keyboard before turning to him. When she did face about her flush was gone. She was again mistress of the situation and said:

"Well, are you ever going to tell me about yourself?"

VB's brows were drawn, and his eyes closed, but before he opened them to look at her a peculiar smile came over his face.

"That man Chopin, and his five-flat prelude —" he said, and stirred with a helpless little gesture of one hand as though no words could convey the appreciation he felt.

"I wonder if you like that as well as I do?" she asked.

He sat forward in his chair and looked hard at her. The constraint was wholly gone; he was seriously intent, thinking clearing, steadily now.

"I used to hear it many times," he said slowly, "and each time I've heard it, it has meant more to me. There's something about it, deep down, covered up by all those big tones, that I never could understand — until now. I guess," he faltered, "I guess I've never realized how much a man has to suffer before he can do a big thing like that. Something about this," — with a gesture of his one hand, — "this house and these hills, and what I've been through out here, and the way you play, helps me to understand what an accomplishment like that must have cost."

She looked at him out of the blue eyes that had become so grave, and said:

"I guess we all have to suffer to do big things; but did you ever think how much we have to suffer to appreciate big things?"

And she went on talking in this strain with a low, even voice, talking for hours, it seemed, while VB listened and wondered at her breadth of view, her sympathy and understanding,

She was no longer a little, sunny-haired girl, a bit of pretty down floating along through life. Before, he had looked on her as such; true, he had known her as sympathetic, balanced, with a keen appreciation of values. But her look, her tone, her insight into somber, grim truths came out with emphasis in the atmosphere created by that music, and to Young VB, Gail Thorpe had become a woman.

A silence came, and they sat through it with

that ease which comes only to those who are in harmony. No constraint now, no flushed faces, no awkward meeting of eyes. The new understanding which had come made even silence eloquent and satisfying.

Then the talk commenced, slowly at first, gradually quickening. It was of many things — of her winter, of her days in the East, of her friends. And through it Gail took the lead, talking as few women had ever talked to him before; talking of personalities, yet deviating from them to deduce a principle here, apply a maxim there, and always showing her humanness by building the points about individuals and the circumstances which surround them.

"Don't you ever get lonely here?" he asked abruptly, thinking that she must have moments of discontent in these mountains and with these people.

"No. Why should I?"

"Well, you've been used to things of a different sort. It seems to be a little rough for a girl — like you."

"And why should n't a nicer community be too fine for a girl like me?" she countered. "I'm of this country, you know. It's mine."

"I had n't thought of that. You're different from these people, and yet," he went on, "you're not like most women outside, either. You've seemed to combine the best of the two extremes. You —"

He looked up to see her gazing at him with a light of triumph in her face. VB never knew, but it was that hour for which she had waited months, ever since the time when she declared to her father, with a welling admiration for the spirit he must have, that he who broke the Captain was a *man*.

Here he was before her, talking personalities, analyzing her! Four months before he would not even linger to say good-by! Surely the spell of her womanhood was on him.

"Oh!" she cried, bringing her hands together. "So you've been thinking about me — what sort of a girl I am, have you?"

Her eyes were aflame with the light of conquest.

Then she said soberly: "Well, it's nice to have people taking you seriously, anyhow."

"That's all any of us want," he answered her; "to be taken seriously, and to be worthy of commanding such an attitude from the people about us. Sometimes we don't realize it until we've thrown away our best chances and then — well, maybe it's too late."

On the words he felt a sudden misgiving, a sudden waning of faith. And, bringing confusion to his ears, was the low voice of this girl-woman saying: "I understand, VB, I understand. And it's never too late to mend!"

Her hand lay in her lap, and almost unconsciously he reached out for it. It came to meet his, frankly, quickly, and his frame was racked by a great, dry sob which came from the depths of his soul.

"Oh, do you understand, Gail?" he whispered doubtfully. "Can you — without knowing?"

He had her hands in both his and strained forward, his face close to hers. The small, firm fingers clutched his hardened ones almost desperately and the blue eyes, so wide now, looking at him so earnestly, were filmed with tears.

"I think I've understood all along," she said, keeping her voice even at the cost of great effort. "I don't know it all — the detail, I mean. I don't need to. I know you've been fighting, VB, nobly, bravely. I know —"

He rose to his feet and drew her up with him, pulling her close to him, closer and closer. One arm slipped down over her shoulders, uncertainly, almost timidly. His face bent toward hers, slowly, tenderly, and she lifted her lips to meet it. It was the great moment of his life. Words were out of place; they would have been puerile, disturbing sounds, a mockery instead of an agency to convey an idea of the strength of his emotions. He could feel her breath on his cheek, and for an instant he hung above her, delaying the kiss, trembling with the tremendous passion within him.

And then he backed away from her — awkwardly, threatening to fall, a limp hand raised toward the girl as though to warn her off.

"Oh, Gail, forgive me!" he moaned. "Not yet! Great God, Gail, I'm not worthy!"

His hoarse voice mounted and he stood backed against the far wall, fists clenched and stiff arms upraised. She took a faltering step toward him.

"Don't!" she begged. "You are — you —"

But he was gone into the night, banging the door behind him, while the girl leaned against her piano and let the tears come.

He was not worthy! He loved; she knew he loved; she had come to meet that great binding, enveloping emotion willingly, frank with the joy of it, as became her fine nature. Then he had run from her, and for her own sake! All the ordeals he had been through in those last months were as brief, passing showers compared with the tempest that raged in him as he rode through the night; and it continued through the hours of light and of darkness for many days. Young VB was a man who feared his own love, and beyond that there can be no greater horror.

He sought solace in the Captain, in driving himself toward the high mark he had set out to attain, but the ideal exemplified in the noble animal seemed more unattainable than ever and he wondered at times if the victory he sought were not humanly impossible. The knowledge that only by conquering himself could he keep his love for Gail Thorpe unsullied never left him, and beside it a companion haunter stalked through and through his consciousness — the fact that they had declared themselves to each other. He was carrying not alone the responsibility of reclaiming his own life; he must also answer for the happiness of a woman!

In those days came intervals when he wondered if this thing were really love. Might it not be something else — a passing hysteria, a reaction from the inner battle? But he knew it was a love stronger than his will, stronger than his great tempter, stronger than the prompting to think of the future when he saw the Thorpe automobile coming up the road that spring day on the first trip the girl had made to the ranch that year. And under the immense truth of the realization he became bodily weak.

Doubt of his strength, too, became more real, more insistent than it had ever been; its hateful power mingled with the thirst, and his heart was rent. What if that love should prove stronger than this discretion which he had retained at such fearful cost, and drag him to her with the stigma he still bore and wreck her!

Gail saw the constraint in him the instant she left the car, and though their handclasp was firm and long and understanding, it sobered her smile.

She tried to start him talking on many things as they sat alone in the log house, but it was useless. He did not respond. So, turning to the subject that had always roused him, that she knew to be so close to his heart, she asked for the Captain.

"In the corral," said VB, almost listlessly. "We'll go out."

So they went together and looked through the gate at the great animal. The Captain stepped close and stretched his nose for Gail to rub, pushing gently against her hand in response.

"Oh, you noble thing!" she whispered to him. "When you die, is all that strength of yours to be wasted? Can't it be given to some one else?"

She looked full on VB, then down at the ground, and said: "You've never told me how you broke the Captain. No one in the country knows. They know that he almost killed you; that you fought him a whole week. But no one knows how. Won't — won't you tell me? I want to know, because it was a real achievement — and *yours.*"

He met her gaze when it turned upward, and for many heartbeats they stood so, looking at each other. Then VB's eyes wavered and he moved a step, leaning on the bars and staring moodily at the stallion.

"It hurts to think about it," he said. "I don't like to remember. That is why I have never told any one. It hurt him and it hurt me."

She waited through the silence that followed for him to go on.

"I've worked and rubbed it and curried it, and nursed the hair to grow over the place. It looks just like a cinch mark now — like the mark of service. No one would ever notice. But it isn't a mark of labor. *I* marked the Captain — I had to do it — had to make him understand me. It laid his side open, and all the nursing, all the care I could give wouldn't make up for it. It's there. The Captain knows it; so do I."

She followed his gaze to the little rough spot far down on the sleek side.

"All wild things have to be broken," she said. "None of them ever become tame of their own volition. And in the breaking a mark is invariably left. The memory hurts, but the mark means nothing of itself, once it is healed. Don't you realize that?

"We all bear marks. The marks of our environment, the marks of our friends, the marks of those we — we love. Some of them hurt for a time, but in the end it is all good. Don't you believe that? We see those who are very dear to us suffer, and it marks us; sometimes just loving leaves its mark. But — those are the greatest things in the world. They're sacred.

"The marks on a woman who goes through fire for a man, say; the marks of a — a mother. They hurt, but in the end they make the bond tighter, more holy."

She waited. Then asked again: "Don't you believe that?"

After a long pause VB answered in a peculiarly bitter voice: "I wish I knew what I believe— if I do believe!"

CHAPTER XVIII

THE LIE

VB'S eyes burned after Gail as she drove away. He followed the car in its flight until it disappeared over the hump in the road; then continued staring in that direction with eyes that did not see — that merely burned like his throat.

Jed came up the gulch with a load of wood, and VB still stood by the gate.

"I never can get used to these here city ways," he grumbled, "no more'n can these ponies."

VB noticed casually that a tug had been broken and was patched with rope.

"Runaway?" he asked, scarcely conscious of putting the question.

"Oh, Bob Thorpe's girl come drivin' her automobile along fit to ram straight through kingdom come, an' don't turn out till she gets so close I thought we was done for; to be sure, I did. Peter, here, took a jump an' busted a tug." He looked keenly at VB. "Funny!" he remarked. "She did n't see me, I know. An' she looked as if she'd been cryin'!"

He could not know the added torture those words carried to the heart of the young fellow battling there silently, covering up his agony, trying to appear at ease.

For the thirst had returned with manifold force, augmenting those other agonies which racked him. All former ordeals were forgotten before the fury of this assault. By the need of stimulant he was subjected to every fiendish whim of singing nerves; from knowing that in him was a love which must be killed to save a woman from sacrifice arose a torment that reached into his very vitals.

The glands of his mouth stopped functioning, and it seemed as though only one thing would take the cursed dryness from his tongue and lips. His fingers would not be still; they kept plucking and reaching out for that hidden chord which would draw him back to himself, or on down into the depths — somehow, he did not care which. Anything to be out of that killing uncertainty!

As he had gained in strength during those months, so it now seemed had the thirst grown. It battered down his spirit, whipped it to a pulp, and dragged it through the sloughs of doubt and despair. His will — did he have a will? He did not know; nor did he seem to care.

It had come — the slipping backward. He had battled well, but now he could feel himself going, little by little, weakening, fighting outwardly but at heart knowing the futility of it all. And going because of Gail Thorpe! "I can't put this mark on her!" he moaned against the Captain's neck. "She said it — that even those we love must bear the mark. And she said it was all good. She was wrong, wrong! Such a thing can't be good!

"Suppose I did keep above it, was sure of myself for a time in a sham way, would n't it only be running the risk of a greater disaster? Would n't it surely come some time? Would n't it, if —

"And then it would kill her, too!"

He hammered the Captain's shoulder with his clenched fist and the great stallion snuggled his cheek closer to the man, trying to understand, trying to comfort.

Then would come moments when his will rallied and Young VB fought with the ferocity of a jungle cat, walking back and forth across the corral, talking to the Captain, condemning his weaker self, gesticulating, promising. At those times he doubted whether it was so much the actual thirst that tore him as it was wondering if he could be worthy of her. Then the old desire would come again, in an engulfing wave, and his fighting would become empty words.

Jed, who had ridden up the gulch to look after a gap in the fence, returned at dusk. As he watched VB feed the Captain he saw in the gloom the straining of the boy's face; heard him talk to the stallion piteously; and the old man's lips framed silent words.

"If it's that girl," he declared, shaking his fist at the skies — "if it's that girl, she ought to be — ought to be spanked. An' if it's th' wantin' of whisky, God pity th' boy!"

THE LIE

Supper was a curious affair. VB tried to help in the preparation but spoiled everything he touched, so far removed was his mind from the work of his hands. Jed ate alone. VB sat down, but could not touch the food offered. He gulped coffee so steaming hot that Jed cried aloud a warning.

"Burned?" scoffed VB. "Burned by that stuff? Jed, you don't know what burning is!"

He got to his feet and paced the floor, one hand pressed against his throat.

The boy sat down twice again and drank from the cup the old man kept filled, but his lips rebelled at food; his hands would not carry it from the plate.

Once Jed rose and tried to restrain the pacing.

"VB, boy," he implored, "set down an' take it easy. Please do! It's been bad before, you know, but it's always turned out good in th' end. It will this time — same as always. Just —"

"Don't, Jed." He spoke weakly, averting his white face and pushing the old man away gently with trembling hands. "You don't understand; you don't understand!"

For the first time he was beyond comfort from the little old man who had showed him the lighted way, who had encouraged and comforted and held faith in him.

After a while a calm fell on VB and he stopped his walking, helped with the work, and then sat, still and white, in his chair. Jed watched him narrowly and comfort came to the old soul, for he believed the boy had won another fight over the old foe; was so sure of it that he whistled as he prepared for the night.

The candle burned on, low against the neck of the bottle, but still bright and steady. VB watched it, fascinated, thought tagging thought through his mind. Then a tremor shot through his body.

"Jed," he said in a voice that was strained but even, "let's play a little pitch, won't you?"

It was his last hope, the last attempt to divert the attack on his will and bolster his waning forces. His nerves jumped and cringed and quivered, but outwardly he was calm, his face drawn to mask the torture.

Jed, aroused, rubbed his sleepy eyes and lighted his pipe. He put on his steel-rimmed spectacles and took down the greasy, cornerless deck of cards to shuffle them slowly, with method, as though it were a rite.

VB sat motionless and a little limp in his chair, too far from the table for comfortable playing. Jed peered at him over his glasses.

"You might get th' coffee beans," he said, with a great yawn.

When the other did not answer he said again: "You might get th' coffee beans, VB. Sleepy?"

The young chap arose then to follow the suggestion, but ignored the query. He went to the cupboard and brought back a handful of the beans, the cowman's poker chips. His hand was waiting for him.

"Good deal?" Jed asked.

VB shook his head. "Not better than a couple."

"O-ho, I'm better off!" and Jed slammed down the ace of hearts.

VB leaned low and played the four-spot, almost viciously, gritting his teeth to force his mind into the game. It rebelled, told him the uselessness of such things, the hopelessness before him, tried to play on the aridness of his throat. But for the moment his will was strong and he followed the game as though gambling for a life.

Suddenly the thought surged through him that he was gambling for a life — his *own* life, and possibly for a woman's life!

Jed made his points, and again, on his own bid, he swept up the coffee counters. Then he took off his glasses and laid them aside with another yawn.

VB wanted to cry aloud to him to keep on playing; he wanted to let Jed Avery know all that the simple, foolish little game of cards meant to him. But somehow his waning faith had taken with it the power to confide.

Jed made four inexcusable blunders in playing that hand, and each time his muttered apologies became shorter. When the hand was over and he had won a point he did not notice that the boy failed to give him the counter.

VB dealt, picked up his cards, and waited for the bid. But Jed's chin was on his breast, one hand lay loosely over the scattered cards before him; the other hung at his side limply. His breath came and went regularly. Sleep had stolen in on VB's final stand!

Oh, if Jed Avery had only known! If his kindly old heart had only read VB better, divining the difference between calm and peace! For a long time VB looked at the old man, his breath gradually quickening, the flame in his eyes growing sharper, more keen, as the consuming fire in him ate away the last barriers of resistance. Once his gaze went to the candle, burning so low against the bottle, yet so brightly, its molten wax running down and adding to the incrustment. He stared wanly at the bright little beacon and shook his head, terror wiping out the vestiges of a smile.

Action! That was what he wanted! Action! He must move or lose his mind and babble and scream! He must move and move rapidly — as rapidly as the rush of those thoughts through his inflamed mind.

He trembled in every limb as he sat there, realizing the need for bodily activity.

And yet, guilefully, craftily, softly, that voice down within him told that action could be of only one sort, could take him only in one direction. It whined and wheedled and gave him a cowardly assurance, made him lie in his own

THE LIE

thoughts; made him cautious in his sneaking determination, for he knew any question Jed might ask would bring frenzy.

VB rose, slowly, carefully, so that there might be no creaking of the boots or scraping of chair legs. He picked up his hat, his muffler, his jumper, and moved stealthily toward the door, opened it inch by inch, and shut it behind him quickly, silently, cutting off the draft of night air — for such a thing might be as disastrous as a cry aloud.

The moon rode above the ridge and the air had lost its winter's edge. It was mild, but with the tang of mountain nights. It was quiet below, but as he stood in the open, pulling on his jumper, he heard the stirring of wind on the points above. It was a soughing, the sort of wind that makes stock uneasy; and VB caught that disquieting vibration.

He stepped out from the cabin and a soft calling from the corral reached him.

"Coming, Captain, coming," he answered.

And with a guilty glance behind him he felt for the gun nestling against his side. His jaw-muscles tightened as he assured himself it was fastened there securely.

The Captain was waiting at the gate. VB let it swing open, then turned and walked toward the saddle rack. The horse followed closely, ears up as though in wonder at this procedure.

"It's all right, Captain," VB whispered as he threw on the saddle blanket. As he drew the cinch tight he muttered: "Or else all wrong!"

Action, action! his body begged. He must have it; nothing else would suffice! He wanted to fly along, skimming the tops of those ghost bushes, ripping through the night, feeling the ripple of wind on that throat, the cooling currents of air against those hammering temples.

And VB knew it was a lie! A rank, deliberate, hypocritical lie! He knew what that action meant, he knew in what direction it would take him. He knew; he knew!

"Oh, Captain!" he sobbed, drawing the bridled head against his chest. "You know what it is to fight! You know what it is to yield! But the yielding did n't break you, boy! It could n't. You were too big, too great to be broken; they could only bend and—"

With a breath of nervous rage he was in the saddle. The Captain's feet rattled on the hard ground with impatience. An instant VB hesitated, gathering the reins, separating them from the strands of thick mane. Then, leaning low, uttering a throaty wail, he gave the Captain his head and into the veiled night they bolted.

The cattle were coming on him, and he was powerless to move! They were bunched, running shoulder to shoulder, and his bed was in their path! Jed tried to raise his arms and could barely move them; his legs rebelled. The stampede was roaring at him! Oh, the rumble of those hoofs, those sharp, cloven, blind, merciless hoofs, that would mangle and tear and trample!

Jed Avery awoke with a start. He was on his feet in the middle of the floor before consciousness came, gasping quickly at the horror of his dream, his excited heart racing!

But it was no stampede. Running hoofs, but no stampede! He stumbled to the door and flung it open. His old eyes caught the flash of a lean, dark object as it raced across the dooryard straight at the gate, never pausing, never hesitating, and taking the bars with a sturdy leap that identified the horse instantly.

"VB!"

He called the name shrilly into the night, but his cry was drowned to the rider's ears, for the Captain's hoofs had caught ground again and were spurning it viciously as he clawed for the speed, the action, that was to satisfy the outraged nerves of his master!

That lie! It was not the action that would satisfy. The flight was only an accessory, an agency that would transport VB to the scene of the renunciation of all that for which he had battled through those long months.

For a long moment Jed stood in the doorway as he had poised at first, stiff, rigid. The sounds of the rushing horse diminuendoed quickly and became only a murmur in the night. Jed Avery's figure lost its tensity, went slack, and he leaned limply against the door frame.

"He's gone!" he moaned. "He's gone! It's broke in on him— Oh, VB, I'm afraid it has! No good takes you south at this time, after th' spell you've had!"

He slammed the door shut and turned back into the room. Unsteady feet took him to his chair, and he settled into it heavily, leaning against the table, his eyes registering the sight of no objects.

"He was fightin' harder'n ever," he whispered dryly, "an' I set here sleepin'. To be sure, I was n't on hand when VB needed me most!"

The ending of his self-accusation was almost a sob, and his head dropped forward. He sat like that for an hour. The fire in the stove went out, and the cool of night penetrated the log walls of the cabin. He gazed unblinkingly at the floor; now and then his lips formed soundless words.

The candle, burning low, fed the flame too fiercely with the last bit of itself. The neck of the bottle was a globule of molten wax in which the short wick swam. The flame had become larger, but it was dead and the smoke rose thickly from its heavy edges. The grease seemed to be disturbed. It quivered, steadied, then settled. The flame slipped down the neck of the bottle and was snuffed out by the confines of the thing.

Jed Avery drew a long, quivering breath, a breath of horror. He turned his face toward the place where the light had been, hoping that his sight had failed. Then he reached out and found the bottle. His hard fingers ran over it, felt the empty neck, paused, and drew away as though it were an infectious thing.

The old man sagged forward to the table, his face in his arms.

CHAPTER XIX

Through the Night

ON into the night went the Captain, bearing VB. Over the gate the bridle-rein drew against his neck and the big beast swung to the right, following the road southward, on down the gulch, on toward Ranger — a fierceness in his rider's heart that was suicidal.

All the bitterness VB had endured, from the stinging torrent his father turned upon him back in New York to the flat realization that to let himself love Gail Thorpe might bring him into worse hells, surged up into his throat and mingled with the craving there. It seeped through into his mind, perverted his thoughts, stamped down the optimism that had held him up, shattered what remnants of faith still remained.

"Faster, Captain!" he cried. "Faster!"

And the stallion responded, scudding through the blue moonlight with a speed that seemed beyond the power of flesh to attain. He shook his fine head and stretched out the long nose as though the very act of thrusting it farther would give more impetus to his thundering hoofs.

VB sat erect in the saddle, a fierce delight aroused by the speed running through his veins like fire — and, reaching to his throat, adding to the scorching. He swung his right hand rhythmically, keeping time to the steady roll of the stallion's feet. The wind tore at him, vibrating his hat brim, whipping the long muffler out from his neck, and he shook his head against it.

He was free at last! Free after those months of doubt, of foolish fighting! He was answering the call that came from the depths of his true self — that hidden self — the call of flesh that needs aid! He cared not for the morrow, for the stretching future. His one thought was on the now — on the rankling, eating, festering moment that needed only one thing to be wiped out forever.

And always, in the back of his mind, was the picture of Gail Thorpe as she had turned from him that afternoon. It loomed large and larger as he tore on to the south through the solitude, ripping his way through the cool murk.

"I won't put my mark on her!" he cried, and whipped the Captain's flanks with his heavy hat, the thought setting his heart flaming. "I won't!" he cried. And again, "I won't!"

He was riding down into his particular depths so to stultify himself that it would be impossible to risk that woman's happiness against the chance that some time, some day, he would go down, loving her, making her know he loved her, but fighting without gain. That, surely, is one sort of love, faulty though the engendering spirit may be.

The whipping with the hat sent the horse on to still greater endeavor. A slight weariness commenced to show in the ducking of his head with every stride, but he did not slacken his pace. His ears were still set stiffly forward, flipping back, one after the other, for word from his rider; the spurn of his feet was still sharp and clear and unfaltering; the spirit in that rippling, dripping body still ran high.

And closing his eyes, drinking the night air through his mouth in great gulps, VB let the animal carry him on and on, — yet backward, back into the face of all that fighting he had summoned, doubling on his own tracks, slipping so easily down the way he had blazed upward with awful sacrifice and hardship.

An hour — two — nine — eleven — the Captain might have been running so a week, and VB would not have known. His mind was not on time, not on his horse. He had ceased to think beyond the recognition of a craving, a craving that he did not fight but encouraged, nursed, teased — for it was going to be satisfied!

The stallion's pace began to slacken. He wearied. The bellows lungs, the heart of steel, the legs of tireless sinew began to feel the strain of that long run. The run waned to a gallop, and the gallop to a trot. There his breathing becoming easier, he blew loudly from his nostrils as though to distend them farther and make way for the air he must have.

VB realized this dully but his heeding of that devilish inner call had taken him so far from his more tender self, from his instinctive desire to love and understand, that he did not follow out his comprehension.

"Go it, boy!" he muttered. "It's all I'll ask of you — just this one run."

And the Captain, dropping an ear back for the word, leaned to the task, resuming the steady, space-eating gallop mile after mile. All the way into Ranger they held that pace. In the last mile the stallion stumbled twice, but after both breaks in his stride ran on more swiftly for many yards, as though to make up to his master for the jolting the half falls gave him. He was a bit unsteady on those feet as he took the turn and dropped down the low bank into the river. They forded it in a shimmer of silver as the horse's legs threw out the black water to be frozen and burnished by the light of the moon. The stallion toiled up the far bank at a lagging trot, and on the flat VB pulled the panting animal down to a walk.

Oh, VB, it was not too late then, had you only realized it! Your ideal was still there, more exemplary than ever before, but you could not recognize it through those eyes which saw only the red of a wrecking passion! You had drained to the last ounce of reserve the strength of that spirit you had so emulated, which had been as a shining light, an unfaltering candle in the darkness. It was stripped bare before you as that splendid animal gulped between breaths. Could you have but seen! Could something only have *made* you see! But it was not to be.

VB had forgotten the Captain. In the face of his wretched weakening the stallion became merely a conveyance, a convenience, a means for stifling the neurotic excitement within him. He forgot that this thing he rode represented his only achievement — an achievement such as few men ever boast.

He guided the stallion to a half-wrecked log house south of the road, dismounted, and stood a moment before the shack, his glittering eyes on the squares of light yonder under the rising hill. He heard a faint tinkling from the place, and a voice raised in laughter.

As he watched, a mounted man passed between him and the yellow glare. In a moment he saw the man enter the saloon door.

"Come, boy," he muttered, moving cautiously through the opening into the place. "You'll be warm in here. You'll cool off slowly."

Then, in a burst of hysterical passion, he threw his arms about the stallion's head and drew it to him fiercely.

"Oh, I won't be gone long, Captain!" he promised. "Not long — just a little while. It's not the worst, Captain! I'm not weakening!"

Drunk with the indulgence of his nervous weakness, he lied glibly, knowing he lied, without object—just to lie, to pervert life. And as the Captain's quick, hot breath penetrated his garments, VB drew the head still tighter.

"You're all I've got, Captain," he muttered, now in a trembling calm. "You'll wait. I know that. I know what you will do better than I know anything else in the world — better than I know what -- what *I'll* do! Wait for me, boy — wait right here!"

His voice broke on the last word as he stumbled through the door and set off toward the building against the hill. He did not hear the Captain turn, walk as far as the door of the shack, and peer after him anxiously. Nor did he see the figure of a man halted in the road, watching him go across the flat, chaps flapping, brushing through the sage noisily.

VB halted in the path of light, swaying the merest trifle from side to side as he pulled his chap belt in another hole and tried to still the twitching of his hands, the weakening of his knees.

The tinkling he had heard became clear. He could see now. A Mexican squatted on his spurs, back against the wall, and twanged a fandango on a battered guitar. His hat was far back over his head, cigarette glowing in the corner of his mouth, gay blue muffler loose on his shoulders. He hummed to the music, his voice rising now and then to float out into the night above the other sounds from the one room.

The bar of rough boards, top covered with red oilcloth, stretched along one side. Black bottles flashed their high lights from a shelf behind it, above which hung an array of antlers. The bartender, broad Stetson shading his face, talked loudly, his hands wide apart on the bar and bearing much of his weight. Now and then he dropped his head to spit between his forearms.

Three men in chaps lounged before the bar, talking. One, the tallest, talked with his head flung back and gestures that were a trifle too loose. The shortest looked into his face with a ceaseless, senseless smile, and giggled whenever the voice rose high or the gestures became unusually wild. The third, elbows on the oilcloth, head on his fists, neither joined in nor appeared to heed the conversation.

Back in the room stood two tables, both covered with green cloth. One was unused; the other accommodated four men. Each of the quartet wore a hat drawn low over his face; each held cards. They seldom spoke; when they did, their voices were low. VB saw only their lips move. Their motions were like the words — few and abrupt. When chips were counted it was with expertness; when they were shoved to the center of the table it was with finality.

Near them, tilted against the wall in a wire-trussed chair, sat a sleeping man, hat on the floor.

Two swinging oil lamps lighted the smoke-fogged air of the place, and their glow seemed to be diffused by it, idealizing everything, softening it —

Everything except the high lights from the bottles on the shelf. Those were stabs of searing brightness; they hurt VB's eyeballs.

His gaze traveled back to the Mexican. The melody had drifted from the fandango into a swinging waltz song popular in the cities four years before. He whistled the air through his teeth. The cigarette was still between his lips. The face brought vague recollections to VB. Then he remembered that this was Julio, the Mexican who ran with Rhues. He belonged to Rhues, they had told him, body and soul.

Thought of Rhues sent VB's right hand to his left side, up under the arm. He squeezed the gun that nestled there.

Of a sudden, nausea came to the man who looked in. It was not caused by fear of Rhues — of the possibility of an encounter. The poignant fumes that came from the open door stirred it, and the sickness was that of a man who sees his great prize melt away.

For the moment VB wanted to rebel. He tore his eyes from those glittering bottles; tried to stop his breathing that treacherous nostrils might not inhale those odors.

But it was useless — his feet would not carry him away. He knew he must move, move soon, and though he now cried out in his heart against it he knew which way his feet would carry him.

He half turned his body and looked back toward the shack where the Captain waited, and a tightening came in his throat to mingle with the rapaciousness there.

"Just a little while, Captain," he whispered, feeling childishly that the horse would hear the words and understand. "Just a little while — I'm just — just going to take a little hand in the card game."

And as the Mexican finished his waltz with a rip of the thumb clear across the six strings of his instrument, Young VB put a foot on the threshold of the saloon and slowly drew himself to his full height in the doorway. Framed by darkness he stood there, thumbs in his belt, mouth in a grim line, hat down to hide the pallor of his cheeks, the torment in his eyes; his shoulders were braced back in resolution, but his knees, inside his generous chaps, trembled.

CHAPTER XX

THE LAST STAND

EVEN the vibrating guitar strings seemed to be stilled suddenly. For VB, an abrupt hush crushed down on the scene. He felt the eyes as, pair after pair, they followed those of the Mexican and gazed at him; even the man slumbering in his chair awoke, raised his head, and stared at him sleepily. He stood in the doorway, leaning lightly against the logs, returning each gaze in turn.

"Hello, VB!" one of the trio before the bar said.

"Hello, Tom!" answered the newcomer — and stepped into the room.

Then what hush had fallen — real or imaginary — lifted and the talk went on, the game progressed.

Perhaps the talk was not fully sincere, possibly the thoughts of the speakers were not always on their words, for every man in the place stole glances at the tall young fellow as he moved slowly about the room.

They had known for months the fight that was going on up there on Jed Avery's ranch. They knew that the man who had mastered the Captain and set his name forever in the green annals of the country had been fighting to command himself against the attacks of the stuff they peddled here in the saloon at Ranger. They knew how he had fought off temptation, avoided contact with whisky — and now, late at night, he had walked slowly into the heart of the magnet that had exerted such an influence on him. So they watched VB as he moved about.

The sharp lights from those black bottles! Like snakes' eyes, they commanded his — and, when this power had been exerted, they seemed to stab the brain that directed sight at them. In the first few steps across the rough floor VB answered their call to look a half dozen times, and after each turning of his gaze jerked his eyes away in pain.

He did not turn toward the bar — rather, kept close to the wall, passing so near the squatting Mexican that the flap of his chaps brushed the other's knees. The Greaser picked at the strings of his instrument aimlessly, striking unrelated chords, tinkling on a single string; then came a few bars from the fandango. His head was tilted to one side and a glittering eye followed the slow-moving figure of Young VB.

By the time the newcomer was halfway toward the poker table the Mexican got to his feet, sliding his back slowly up the wall until he reached a standing position. Then, for the first time taking his eyes from VB, he stepped lightly toward the door. After a final tinkling chord had fallen he disappeared, guitar slung under one arm, walking slowly away from the lighted place. But when he was beyond sight of those within, he ran.

VB went on, past the just-awakened man in his chair, close to the poker table. The players looked up again, first one, with a word of recognition; then two spoke at once, and after he had raked in the pot the fourth nodded with a welcoming grunt.

The young fellow leaned a shoulder against the log wall and watched the game. That is, he looked at it. But continually his fevered memory retained a vision of those glares from the bottles.

His mind again played crazy tricks, as it always did when the thirst clamored loudly. The rattle of the chips sounded like ice in glasses, and he turned his head quickly toward the bar, following the imaginary sound.

The four men there were just drinking. He followed their movements with wild eyes. The bartender lifted his glass to the level of his forehead in salute, then drained its contents slowly, steadily, every movement from the lifting to the setting down of the empty glass smooth, deliberate — even polished — the movements of a professedly artful drinker. The silent man offered no good word — merely lifted the glass and drank, tipping his head but slightly, emptying the glass with an uneven twisting of the wrist, something like an exaggerated tremble. The short man tossed his drink off by elevating the glass quickly to his lips and throwing his head back with a jerk to empty it into his mouth. The tall man, who talked loudly and motioned much, waved his drink through the air to emphasize a declaration, and with an uncertain swoop directed it to his lips. He leaned backward from the hips to drink, and the movement made him reel and grasp the bar for support.

As he had followed the movements of those men, so VB followed the course of the stuff they drank down their throats; in imagination, down *his* throat, until it hit upon and glossed over that spot which wailed for soothing!

Oh, how he wanted it! Still, all those months of battling had not been without result. The rigid fight he had made carried him on, even in face of his resolve to yield, and he delayed, put it off just a moment — lying to himself!

He turned back to the game.

"Sit in, VB?" one of the players asked.

"Don't mind."

He dragged another chair to the table, unbuttoned and cast off his jumper, gave the hat another low tug, and tossed a yellow-backed twenty to the table. The chips were shoved toward him.

"Jacks or better," the dealer said, and shot the cards about the board.

VB won a pot. He bet eagerly on the next and lost. Then he won again. The game interested him for the moment.

"Oh, just one more li'l' drink!" cried the garrulous cowboy at the bar.

VB had passed the opening, went in later, drew three cards, failed to help his tens, and hiked the bet' Called, he dropped the hand; and the winner, showing aces up, stared at the boy who had bet against openers on lone tens. He noticed that VB's hands trembled, and he wondered. He could not feel VB's throat. Nor could he hear the careless plea of the sotted rider for just one more drink ringing in VB's burning brain.

A big pot was played and the winner, made happy, said:

"Well, I'll buy a drink."

The bartender, hearing, came to the table.

"What'll it be?" he asked.

"Whisky," said the man on VB's right, and the word went around the circle.

Then a moment's pause, while the cards fluttered out.

"VB?"

There it was, reaching out for him, holding out its tentacles that ceased to appear as such and became soft, inviting arms. It was that for which he had ridden through the night; it was that against which he had fought month after month until, this night, he realized that a fight was useless; it was the one solace left him, for indirectly it had brought into his life the glorious thing — and wiped it out again. So why hold off? Why refuse?

But those months of fighting! He could not overcome that impetus which his subjective self had received from the struggle. Consciously he wanted the stuff — oh, how he wanted it! But deep in him *something* —

"Not now — thanks," he managed to mutter, and clasped his cards tightly.

The bartender turned away, rubbing his chin with one finger, as though perplexed. VB dealt, and with lightning agility. He even broke in on the silence of the playing with senseless chatter when the drinks were brought. He held his cards high that he might not see the glasses, and was glad that the men did not drink at once. Nor did they drink for many moments. The opener was raised twice; few cards were drawn. A check passed one man, the next bet, the next raised, and VB, the deal, came in.

The opener raised again and the bartender, seeing, stepped across to watch. The drowsy lounger, sensing the drift of the game, rose to look on.

VB dropped out. He held threes, but felt that they had no place in that game. The betting went on and on, up and up, three men bent on raising, the fourth following, intent on having a look, anyhow. VB threw his cards down and dropped his hands loosely on the table. The back of his right hand touched a cold object. He looked down quickly. It was resting against a whisky glass.

"And ten more," a player said.

"Ten — and another ten." More chips rattled into the pile.

His hand stole back and hot fingers reached out to touch with sensitive tips that cool surface. His nostrils worked to catch the scent of the stuff. His hand was around the glass.

"I'm staying."

"You are — for five more."

VB's fingers tightened about the thing, squeezed it in the palm of his hand. It had felt cool at first; now it was like fire. The muscles of that arm strove to lift it. His inner mind struggled, declared against the intention, weakened, yielded, and —

"Well, I'm through. Fight it out."

The man at VB's right dropped his cards in disgust and with a quick movement reached for his drink.

His nervous, hot hand closed on VB's and their surprised glances met.

"Excuse me," muttered VB.

"Sure!" said the other, surly over his lost stake, and gulped down the whisky.

Two of the players went broke in that pot. The fourth had a scant remnant of his original stack left, and VB was loser. The two who had failed shoved back their hats and yawned, almost simultaneously.

"How about it?" asked the winner, stacking his chips.

16

"I'm satisfied," said the man at VB's right.

"And VB?"

"Here, too!"

The boy sat back in his chair with a long-drawn breath after shoving his chips across to be cashed. He pushed his hat back for the first time, and a man across the table stared hard as he saw the harried face. The others were busy, cashing in.

"Just get in, VB?" some one asked.

He heard the question through a tumult. His muscles had already contracted in the first movement of rising; his will already directed his feet across the room to the bar to answer the call of those searching bottle eyes. Inwardly he raged at himself for holding off so long, for wasting those months, for letting that other new thing come into his life only to be torn away again; when it all meant mere delay, a drawing out of suffering! Only half consciously he framed the answer:

"Yes, I rode down to-night."

"Goin' on out?"

"What?" he asked, forcing his mind to give heed to the other.

"Goin' on out, or goin' to hang around a while?"

"I don't know." The boy got to his feet, and the reply was given with rare bitterness. "I don't know," he said again, voice mounting. "I may go out — and I may not. I may hang around a while, and it may n't take long. I'm

THE LAST STAND

here to finish something I started a long time ago, something that I've been putting off. I'm going to put a stop to a lying, hypocritical existence. I'm —"

He broke off thickly and moved away from the table.

No imagination created a hush this time. On his words the counting of chips ceased. They looked at him, seeing utter desperation, and not understanding.

A face outside that had been pressed close to a window was lowered, darkness hiding the glitter of green eyes and the leering smile of triumph. A figure slunk along carefully to the corner of the building and joined two others.

It was his chance! Rhues was out to get his man this moonlight night, and there was now no danger. Young VB was no longer afraid to take a drink. He would give up his fight, give up his hard-wrung freedom, and when drunken men go down, shot in a quarrel, there is always cause. He had him now!

VB lurched across the room toward the bar. In mid-floor he paused, turned, and faced those at the poker table.

"Don't mistake me," he said with a grin. "Don't think I'm talking against any man in the country. It's myself, boys — just *me*. I'm the liar, the hypocrite. I've tried to lie myself into being what I never can be. I've come out here among you to go by the name of the outfit I ride for. You don't know me, don't even know my name, say nothing of my own rotten self. Well, you're going to know me as I am."

He swung around to face the bar. The bartender pulled nervously on his mustache.

"What'll it be, VB?" he asked, surprised knowledge sending the professional question to his lips.

"The first thing you come to," the boy muttered, and grasped the bar for support.

CHAPTER XXI

Guns Crash

OUT in the shadow of the building three men huddled close together, talking in whispers — Rhues, Matson, and the Mexican. Rhues had watched the progress of the poker game, waiting the chance he had tried to seek out ever since that day up at Avery's when he had been beaten down by the flailing fists of that tall young tenderfoot. He had seen VB start for the bar; he knew the hour had struck.

"We've got him!" he whispered. "He won't get away this time. They won't be no mistakes."

"S-s-s-s!" the Greaser warned.

"Aw, nobody'll ever know," Rhues scoffed in an undertone. "They'll never know that unless you spill. An' if you do — it'll mean three of us to th' gallows, unless — we're lynched first!"

Silence a moment, and they heard VB's voice raised. Then Rhues whispered his quick plans.

"Take it easy," he warned in conclusion. "Don't start nothin'. Let him git drunk; then he'll do th' startin' an' it'll be easy."

Inside a bottle was thumped on the bar, a glass beside it. Feverishly VB reached for both, lifting the glass with uncertain hand, tilting the bottle from the bar, not trusting his quaking muscles to raise it. The neck touched the glass with a dull clink; the mouth of the bottle gurgled greedily as the first of the liquor ran out — for all the world as if it had waited these months for that chuckle of triumph.

And then that romanticism of youth came to the surface of his seething thoughts again. It would be the closing of a chapter, that drink. It was for her sake he would lift it to his lips. He wanted to bid her a last, bitter farewell. She was over there, far across the hills, sleeping and dreaming — with her golden hair — over there in the northeast. He laughed harshly, set the bottle back on the bar, and turned his face in her direction.

Those who watched from the other end of the room saw him turn his head unsteadily; saw the sudden tenseness which spread through his frame, stiffening those faltering knees. He turned slowly toward the door and thrust his face forward as though to study and make certain that he saw rightly.

Like a rush of fire the realization swept through him. A man stood there in the moonlight, and the sheen from the heavens was caught on the dull barrel of a gun in his hand.

VB was covered, and he knew by whom! The man who had fought less than half a dozen times in his life, and then with bare fists, was the object of a trained gun hand. He could almost see the glitter of the green eyes that were staring at him.

Instinct should have told him to spring to one side; a leap right or left would have carried him out of range, but instinct had been warped by all those months of struggle.

He was on the brink, at the point of losing his balance; but the battling spirit within him still throbbed, though his frenzy, his lack of faith, had nearly killed it. Now the thing came alive pulsing, bare!

An instant before he had not cared what happened. Now he did, and the end was not the only thing in view; the means counted with Young VB.

He did not jump for shelter. He roared his rage as he prepared to stand and fight.

The others understood before his hand reached his shirt front. The bartender dropped behind the fixture and the others in the room sprang behind the barrels and stove. By the time VB's hand had clasped the neck of his shirt he stood alone. When the vicious yank he gave the garment ripped it open from throat halfway to waist the first belch of fire came from that gun out there.

The bottle on the bar exploded, fine bits of glass shooting to the far corners of the room.

"Come on — you — yellow —"

VB's fingers found the butt of his Colt, closed and yanked. It came from the holster, poised, muzzle upward, his thumb over the hammer. Possibly he stood thus a tenth part of a second, but while he waited for his eyes to focus well a generation seemed to parade past. He was hunted down by a crawling piece of vermin!

A parallel sprang to his mind. While Rhues sought his body did not another viper seek his soul? Was —

Then he made out the figure — crouched low. The forty-five came down, and the room resounded with its roar. He stood there, a greenhorn who had never handled a weapon in his life until the last year, giving battle to a gun fighter whose name was a synonym!

Out of the moonlight came another flash, and before VB could answer the hunched figure had leaped from the area framed by the doorway.

"You won't stand!" the boy cried, and strode across the room.

"Don't be a fool! VB!"

The bartender's warning might as well have been unheard. Straight for the open door went the boy, gun raised, coughing from the powder smoke. But the mustached man, though panderer by profession, revolted at unfairness; perhaps it was through the boy's ignorance, but he knew VB walked only to become a target. Twice his gun roared from behind the bar and the two swinging lamps became scattered, tinkling fragments.

VB seemed not to heed, not to notice that he was in darkness. He reached the door, put his left hand against the casing, and looked out.

With lights behind he would have been riddled on the instant. But, looking from blackness to moonlight, he was invisible for the moment — but only for a moment.

The stream of yellow stabbed at him again and Young VB, as though under the blow of a sledge, spun round and was flattened against the wall.

His left breast seemed to be in flames. He reached for it, fired aimlessly with the other hand in the direction of his hidden foe, and let the gun clatter to the floor.

He wondered if it were death — that darkness. He felt the fanning of the wind, heard, dimly, its uneasy soughing. It was very dark.

A movement and its consequent grip of pain brought him back. He saw then that a heavy cloud, wind driven, had blotted out the moon. In a frenzy he came alert! He was wounded! He had dropped his gun and they were waiting for him out there, somewhere; waiting to finish him!

He could feel the smearing of blood across his chest as his clothing held it in. His legs commenced to tremble, from true physical weakness this time.

And the Captain was waiting!

That thought wiped out every other; he was possessed with it. He might be dying, but if he could only get to the Captain; if he could only feel that silken nose against his cheek! Nothing would matter then.

If he could get up, if he could mount, the Captain would take care of him. He could outrun those bullets — the Captain. He would take him home, away from this inferno.

"I'm coming, Captain!" he muttered brokenly. "You're waiting! Oh, I know where to find you. I'm coming, boy, coming!"

He stepped down from the doorway and reeled, a hand against his wounded breast. It seemed as though it required an eternity to regain his balance. Then he lurched forward a step. Oh, they were merciless! They opened on him from behind — when he had no weapon, when his life was gushing away under his shirt! Those shots never came from one gun alone. More than one man fired on him!

His salvation then was flight. He ran, staggering, stumbling. He plunged forward on his face and heard a bullet scream over him.

"Oh, Captain!" he moaned. "Can't you come and get me? Can't you?"

He snarled his determination to rally those senses that tried to roam off into vagaries. He got to his hands and knees and crawled, inch by inch. He heard another shot, but it went wild. He got to his feet and reeled on. They thought they'd done for him when he fell! He heard himself laughing crazily at the joke.

"Oh, you'll laugh, too — Captain!" he growled. "It's a joke — you'll — if I can only get to — you!"

His numb, lagging legs seemed to make conscious efforts to hold him back. His head became as heavy as his feet and rolled about on his neck, now straight forward, now swinging from side to side. His arms flopped as no arm ever should flop. And he heard the blood bubbling under his vest. Perhaps he would never get there! Perhap she was done for!

"Oh, no — I can't quit before — I get to — you, Captain!" he muttered as he fell again. "You're waiting — where I told you to wait! I've got to — get — there!"

Of only one thing in this borderland between consciousness and insensibility was he certain — the Captain was waiting. The Captain was waiting! If he could get that far — It was the climax of all things. To reach his horse; to touch him; to put his arms about those ankles as he fell and hold them close; to answer trust with trust. For through all this the Captain had waited!

The shack where he had left the horse swam before his eyes. He heard the breath making sounds in his throat as he crawled on toward it, counting each hand-breadth traveled an achievement. He tried to call out to the horse, but the words clogged and he could not make his voice carry.

"Just a moment, boy!" he whispered. "Only — a moment longer — then you won't have — to wait!"

He was conscious again that his pursuers fired from behind. It was moonlight once more, and they could see him as he reeled on toward the shack. He sprawled again as his foot met a stone, and the guns ceased to crash.

But VB did not think on this more than that instant. He found no comfort in the cessation of firing. For him, only one attainable object remained in life. He wanted to be with the thing of which he was certain, away from all else — to know a faith was justified; to sense once again stability!

His hand struck rough wood. He strained his eyes to make out the tumble-down structure rising above him.

"Captain!" he called, forcing his voice up from a whisper. "Come — boy, I'm — ready — to go — home!"

Clinging to the logs, he raised himself to his feet and swayed in through the door.

"Captain," he muttered, closing his eyes almost contentedly and waiting. "Captain?"

He started forward in alarm, a concern mounting through his torture and dimming his sensibilities.

"Captain — are you — here?"

He stumbled forward, arms outstretched in the darkness, feeling about the space. He ran into a wall; turned, met another.

"Captain!" he cried, his voice mounting to a ranting cry.

The Captain was gone!

Reason for keeping on slipped from VB's mind. He needed air, so his reflexes carried him through the doorway again, out of the place where he had left the stallion, out of the place where his trust had been betrayed. He stumbled, recovered his balance, plunged on out into the moonlight, into the brush, sobbing heavily. His knees failed. He crashed down, face plowing into cool soil.

"Captain"! he moaned. "Oh, boy — I did n't think — *you* would — fail — No wonder — I could n't keep — going —"

He did not hear the running feet, did not know they rolled him over, Rhues with his gun upraised.

"I got him, th' ——" he muttered.

"Then let's get out — *pronto!*"

Twenty minutes later a man with a lantern stepped out of the shack in which the Captain had stood. Two others were with him.

"Yes, he left his horse there, all right," the man with the light muttered. "He got to him an' got away. Nobody else could lead that horse off. He could n't 'a' been hard hit or he could n't 'a' got up."

CHAPTER XXII

TABLES TURN; AND TURN AGAIN

A YOUNG chap from the East who was in Clear River County because of his lungs named her Delilah when she was only a little girl — Delilah Gomez. She cooked now for the Double Six Ranch, the buildings of which clustered within a stone's throw of the Ranger post office. And that night as she sat looking from her window she thought, as she did much of the time, about the smiling Julio with his guitar — the handsome fellow who lived with Señor Rhues and did no work, but wore such fine chaps and kerchiefs!

She sighed, then started to her feet as she saw him come through the gate and up the path, and hastened to open the door for him.

Julio took off his hat.

"It is late," he said, flashing his teeth. "I come to ask you to do something for me, Delilah."

"What is it — now — so late?" she asked breathlessly.

"In the old house across the road" — he pointed — "is a horse. It is the horse of a friend. A friend, also, of Señor Rhues. He is now in the saloon. He is drunk. Will you take the horse away? To the place of Señor Rhues? And put him in the barn? And be sure to fasten the door so he will not get out?"

Delilah was puzzled a moment.

"But why," she asked, "why so late?"

Julio bowed profoundly again.

"We go — Señor Rhues, Señor Matson, and I, Julio, to take our friend away from the saloon. We are busy. Señor Rhues offers this."

He pressed a dollar into her palm. And for the dollar and a flash of Julio's teeth, Delilah went forth upon her commission.

The three men watched her go.

"That devil'd tear a man to pieces," Rhues muttered. "Any woman can handle him, though. Git him locked up, an' th'—— tenderfoot can't make it away! He'll have to stay an' take what's comin'!"

The girl led the Captain down the road, past the Double Six Ranch, on to the cramped little barn behind the cabin where lived Rhues and his two companions.

It was not an easy task. The Captain did not want to go. He kept stopping and looking back. But the girl talked to him kindly and stroked his nose and — VB himself had taught him to respect women. This woman talked softly and petted him much, for she remembered the great horse she had seen ridden by the tall young fellow. Besides, the dollar was still in her hand. She led him into the cramped little barn, left him standing and came out, closing the doors behind her. Then she set out for home, clasping the dollar and thinking of Julio's smile.

The first shot attracted her. The second alarmed, and those that followed terrified the girl. She ran from the road and hovered in the shadow of a huge bowlder, watching fearfully, uttering little moans of fright.

She heard everything. Some men ran past her in the direction of Rhues's cabin, and she thought one of them must be Julio. But she was too frightened to stir, to try to determine; too frightened to do anything but make for her own home.

The girl moved stealthily through the night, facing the moon that swung low, unclouded again, making all radiant. She wanted to run for home, where she could hide under blankets, but caution and fear held her to a walk. She did not cry out when she stumbled over the body; merely cowered holding both hands over her lips.

For a long time she stood by it, looking down, not daring to stoop, not daring to go away. Then the hand that sprawled on the dirt raised itself fell back; the lips parted, a moan escaped, and the head rolled from one side to the other.

The fear of dead things that had been on her passed. She saw only a human being who was hurt. She dropped to her knees and took the head in her lap.

"Oh, *por Dios!* It is the *señor* who rode the horse!" she muttered, and looked quickly over her shoulder at the Rhues cabin.

"They left him; they thought he was dead," she went on aloud. "They should know; he should be with them. They were going for him when the shooting began!"

She looked closer into VB's face and he moaned again. His eyes opened. The girl asked a sharp question in Spanish.

"Is the *señor* much hurt?" she repeated in the language he understood.

"Oh, Captain!" he moaned. "Why? Why did you — quit?"

She lifted him up then and he struggled sluggishly to help himself.

Once he muttered: "Oh, Gail! It hurts so!"

She strained to the limits of her lithe strength until she had him on his feet. Then she drew one of his arms about her neck, bracing herself to support his lagging weight.

"Come," she said comfortingly. "We will go — to them."

No light showed from the Rhues cabin, but the girl was sure the men were there, or would come soon. Loyal to Julio for the dollar and the memory of his graciousness, she worked with the heart of a good Samaritan, guiding the unconscious steps of the muttering man toward the little dark blot of houses.

It was a floundering progress. Twice in the first few rods the man went down and she was sorely put to get him on his feet again. But the moving about seemed to bring back his strength, and gradually he became better able to help himself.

They crossed the road and passed through the gap in the fence by the cabin. VB kept muttering wildly, calling the girl Gail, calling for the Captain in a plaintive voice.

"There they are now! See the light?" she whispered. "It is not much. They have covered the window. Yes."

"What?" VB asked, drawing a hand across his eyes.

She repeated her assertion that the men were in the cabin and he halted, refusing drunkenly to go on.

"No," he said, shaking his head. "I'm unarmed — they —"

But she tugged at him and forced him to go beside her. They progressed slowly, painfully, quietly. There was no sound, except VB's hard breathing, for they trod in dust. They approached the house and the girl put out a hand to help her along with the burden.

A thin streak of light came from a window. It seemed to slash deeply into the staggering man, bringing him back to himself. Then a sound, the low, worried nickering of a horse! The Mexican girl felt the arm about her neck tighten and tremble.

"The Captain!" VB muttered, looking about wildly.

He opened his lips to cry out to the horse as

the events of the night poured back into his consciousness, to cry his questioning and his sorrow, to put into words the mourning for a faith, but that cry never came from his throat.

The nickering of the stallion and the flood of memory had brought him to a clear understanding of the situation; a sudden glare of light from the abruptly uncovered window before which he and the girl stood provoked an alertness which was abnormally keen, that played with the subjective rather than the more cumbersome objective. He stooped with the quickness of a drop and scuttled into the shadows, cautious, the first law of man athrob.

The man who had brushed away the blanket that had screened the window burst into irritated talk. VB recognized him as Matson. Back in the shadows of the room he saw the Mexican standing.

A table was close to the window, so close that in crowding behind it Matson had torn down the blanket that had done service as a curtain. A lamp burned on the table, its wick so high that smoke streamed upward through the cracked chimney. And close beside the lamp, eyes glittering, cruel cunning in every line, the flush of anger smearing it, was the face of Rhues!

VB, crouching there, saw then that Matson's finger was leveled at Rhues.

"It ain't good money!"

That was the declaration Matson had made as

the blanket slipped down and disclosed the scene. He repeated it, and his voice rose to a snarl.

Delilah started to rise but VB jerked her back with a vehemence that shot a new fear through the girl, that made her breathe quickly and loudly. For the first time he turned and looked at the girl, not to discover who this might be that had brought him to the nest of those who sought his life, but to threaten.

"You stay here," he whispered sharply. "If you make a sound, I'll — you'll never forget it!"

His face was close to hers and he wagged his head to emphasize the warning.

Where she had expected to find a friend the Mexican girl realized that she had encountered a foe. Where she had, from the fullness of her heart and for a dollar and the admiration of Julio, sought to help, she knew now that she had wronged. His intensity filled her with this knowledge and sent her shrinking against the wall of the cabin, a hand half raised to her cheek, trembling, wanting to whimper for mercy.

"Keep still!" he warned again, and, stretching one hand toward her as though to do sentry duty, ready to throttle any sound, to stay any flight, to bolster his commands, he crept closer to the window.

"Why ain't it good?" Rhues was asking in a voice that carried no great conviction, as though he merely stalled for time.

VB saw him stretch a bill close to the lamp

and Matson lean low beside him. The light fell on the piece of currency, not six feet from VB's fever-bright eyes. He saw that they were inspecting a fifty-dollar bill issued by the Confederate States of America! And Rhues said grudgingly: "Well, if that ain't good, they's only six hunderd 'n all!"

Up came the buried memories, struggling through all the welded events in the furnace consciousness of the man who pressed his face so close to the window's crinkly glass. His eyes sought aimlessly for some object that might suggest a solution for the slipping thought he tried to grasp. They found it — found it in a rumpled, coiled contrivance of leather that lay beside the lamp. It was a money belt. The money belt that Kelly, the horse buyer, had worn!

Six hundred dollars! And a Confederate States fifty-dollar bill! They were quarreling over the spoils of that chill murder!

VB swayed unsteadily as he felt a rage swell in him, a rage that nullified caution. He turned his eyes back to the Mexican girl cringing just out of his reach and moved the extended hand up and down slowly to keep his warning fresh upon her. He wanted time to think, just a moment to determine what action would be most advisable. His heart raced unevenly and he thought the hot edges of his wound were blistering.

"That's two hundred apiece, then," Rhues said, and straightened.

VB saw that the hand which had dropped the worthless piece of paper held a roll of yellow-backed bills.

"Two hundred we all git," he growled. "You git it, Julio gits it, I git it — an' I'm th' party what done th' work!"

VB stooped and grasped Delilah roughly by the arm. He held a finger to his lips as he dragged the shaking girl out to where she could see.

"Watch!" he commanded, close in her ear. "Watch Rhues — and the others!"

Rhues counted slowly, wetting his thumb with hasty movements and dropping bills from the roll to the table top.

"Both you" — he looked up to indicate Matson and Julio — "gits 's much 's me, an' I done th' work!"

"An' if we're snagged, we stand as good a chanct o' gettin' away as you," Matson remarked, and laughed shortly.

Rhues looked up again and narrowed the red lids over his eyes.

"You said it!" he snarled. "That's why it's good to keep yer mouths shut! That's why you got to dig out — with me.

"If I'm snagged — remember, they's plenty o' stories I could tell about you two — an' I will, too, if I'm snagged 'cause o' you!"

He worked his shoulders in awkward gesture.

"An' that's why we want our share," Matson growled back. "An' want it quick! We watched th' road; you done th' killin'. We thought it was jus' to settle things with that ——, but it wasn't. It was profitable."

He ended with another short laugh.

"Well, I said I'd git him, did n't I? An' I did, did n't I? An' if th' first time went wrong it was — profitable, was n't it?"

"Yes, but queek, queeker!" the Mexican broke in. "They might come — now!"

"Well, quit snivelin'!" snapped Rhues. "It did n't go as we planned. I had to shoot 'fore I wanted to. But I got him, did n't I?"

Julio reached for the pile of bills Rhues shoved toward him; Matson took his; Rhues pocketed the rest. And outside, VB relaxed his hold on the girl's wrist, raising both hands upward and out, fingers stiff and claw-like.

Kelly, good-natured, careless, likable, trusting Kelly, had gone out to pay toll to this man's viciousness; had gone because he, VB, would not submit to Rhues's bullying! And now they laughed, and called it a profitable mistake!

All his civilized, law-abiding nature rose in its might. All that spirit which demands an eye for an eye, a tooth for a tooth, which makes for statutes and courts and the driving of nations into fixed paths, lifted VB above any caution that the circumstances could have engendered. His whole nature cried out for the justice he had been trained to respect; his single remaining impulse was to make this man Rhues suffer for the act of which there was such ample evidence.

He struggled to find a way toward retribution, for in a moment it might be too late. He had no thought beyond the instant, no idea but to possess himself of something more, to make the case stronger for society. He had seen, he had heard, he had the girl beside him, but he wanted more evidence.

Matson moved away from the window and as he did so the sash sagged inward. It was a hinged casing!

His hands numb from excitement, VB forced his arms against it, shoving stoutly. The force of his effort precipitated his head and shoulders into the room! He had a flash of the three men as they whirled and poised, with oaths, but his mind did not linger on them. His fingers clutched the money belt, drew it to him, and as Rhues dropped a hand to his hip VB staggered backward out of the window, stuffing the money belt inside his shirt, in against the hot wound, and stared about him.

For an instant, silence, as Rhues stood, gun drawn, shoulders forward, gazing at the empty window. Then upon them came a shrill, quavering, anxious cry — the call of the Captain.

CHAPTER XXIII

Life, the Trophy

TO VB, at the sound of the stallion's neighing, came the realization of his position — weaponless in the midst of men who, now of all times, would shoot to kill! His righteous abhorrence of the murder Rhues had done and in which the others had been conspirators did not lessen. He did not falter in his determination for vengeance; but his thirst for it did not detract one whit from his realization of the situation's difficulties.

Seconds were precious. Just a lone instant he poised, looking quickly about, and to his ears came again the cry of the horse, plaintive, worried, appealing.

"Captain!" he cried, and started to run. "Captain! You did n't fail! They *brought* you!"

His voice lifted to a shout as he rounded the corner of the house, and the Captain answered.

With the horse located, VB stumbled across the short intervening space, one hand to his breast doing the double duty of attempting to still the searing of that wound and hold fast to the money belt. He flung himself at the door of the low little stable, jerked the fastening apart, and, backing in, saw men run from the house, heard them curse sharply, and saw them turn and look, each with his shooting hand raised.

VB drew the door shut after him, trembling, thinking swiftly. The Captain nosed him and nickered relief, stepping about in his agitation as though he knew the desperate nature of the corner into which they had been driven.

"We've got to get out, boy," VB cried, running his numb hands over the animal's face in caress. "We're up against it, but there's a way out!"

It was good to be back. It was good to feel that thick, firm neck again, to have the warm breath of the vital beast on his cheek, to sense his dominating presence — for it did dominate, even in that strained circumstance, and in the stress VB found half hysterical joy and voiced it:

"You didn't quit, Captain!" he cried as he felt the cinch hastily. "You didn't quit. They — that woman! She brought you here!"

He flung his arms about the stallion's head in a quick, nervous embrace at the cost of a mighty cutting pain across his chest.

Then the cautious voice of Rhues, outside and close up to the door, talking lowly and swiftly:

"Julio, saddle th' buckskin! Quick! I'll hold him here till we're ready! Then I'll shoot th' —— down in his tracks! We got to ride, anyhow — nothin' 'll make no difference now!"

Raising his voice, Rhues taunted:

"Pray, you ——! Yer goin' to cash!"

VB pressed his face to a crack and saw Rhues in the moonlight, close up to the door. He also saw another man, Julio, leading a horse from the corral on the run. Two other animals, saddled, stood near.

He was cornered, helpless, in their hands — hard hands, that knew no mercy. But he did not give up. His mind worked nimbly, skipping from possibility to possibility, looking, searching for a way out.

He reeled to the black horse and felt the animal's breath against the back of his neck.

"We're up against it, boy," he whispered.

And the voice of Rhues again: "They'll find him to-morrow—with th' belt!"

He broke off sudden'y, as though the words had set in his mind a new idea.

VB did not hear; would not have heeded had his senses registered the words, because an odd apathy had come over him, dulling the pain of his wound, deadening the realization of his danger. He sighed deeply and shook himself and tried to rally, but though a part of him insisted that he gather his faculties and force them to alertness, another tired, lethargic self overbore the warning. Half consciously he pulled the stirrup toward him, put up his foot with an unreal effort, and laboriously drew himself to the saddle. There, he leaned forward on his arms, which were crossed on the Captain's neck, oblivious to all that transpired.

But the great stallion was not insensible to the situation. He could not know the danger, but he did know that he had been led into a strange place, shut there and left virtually a prisoner; that his master had burst in upon him atremble with communicable excitement; that strange voices were raised close to him; that men had been running to and fro; that the sounds of struggling horses were coming from out there; that some man was standing on the other side of the door, closer than most men had ever stood to him. He breathed loudly; then stilled that breath to listen, his head moving with frequent, short jerks as he saw objects move past the cracks in the building. He switched his tail about his hindquarters sharply, and backed a step.

Another voice called softly to Rhues, and Rhues answered:

"Dah! When I rolled him over his holster flopped out of his shirt, empty. He dropped it in th' s'loon. If he 'd had a gun he 'd done fer us 'n there, would n't he?"

Then his voice was raised in a sharp command: "Help him, Julio! Hang on to his ear an' he 'll stand. *Pronto!*"

Sounds of men grunting, of a horse striving to break from them; a sharp cry. These things — and emanating from a scene taking place outside the Captain's sight! He half wheeled and scrubbed the back wall of the stable with his hip, blowing loudly in fright. He stamped a forefoot impatiently; followed that by a brisk, nervous pawing. He tossed his head and chewed his bit briskly; then shook his head and blew loudly again. He shied violently as a man ran past the door, wheeled, crashed into the wall again and, crouching, quivered violently.

VB moaned with pain. When the horse under him had shied the boy had pushed himself erect in the saddle and the effort tore at the wound in his chest. The pain roused him, and as the Captain again wheeled, frantic to find a way out of this pen, VB's heels clapped inward to retain his seat, the spurs drove home, and with a whimper the horse reared to his hind legs, lunged forward, and the front hoofs, shooting out, crashed squarely against the closed door!

Under the force of the blow the door swept outward, screaming on its rusty hinges. A third of the way open it struck resistance, quivered, seemed to hesitate, then continued on its arc.

A surprised, muffled shout, the sound of a body striking ground, a shot, its stream of fire spitting toward the night sky. Then the vicious smiting of hoofs as the Captain, bearing his witless rider, swung in a short circle and made for the river.

Rhues, caught and knocked flat by the bursting open of the door, was perhaps a half-dozen seconds in getting to his feet. He came up shooting, a stream of leaden missiles shrieking aimlessly off into space. Julio and Matson, busy with the refractory buckskin, heard the crash and creak of the swinging door, heard the shout, heard the shot; they turned to see the black stallion sweep from the little building and swirl past them, ears back, teeth gleaming, and bearing to the north.

Still clinging to the buckskin's head, the Mexican drew his gun; Matson, utterly bewildered, fearful of impending consequences, gave the cinch a final tug, but before Julio could fire the water of the river was thrown in radiant spray as the Captain floundered into midstream with VB low on his neck.

Then Rhues was on them, putting into choking words the vileness of his heart. He did not explain beyond:

"Th' —— horse! Th' door got me!"

He seized the cheek strap of the buckskin's bridle and swung up, while the others watched the horse running out into the moonlit river. The pony reared and pivoted on his hind legs.

"Git on yer hosses!" Rhues screeched, yanking at the bit. "He can't git away, with his hoss run down once to-night! An' if we let him — we swing!"

Goaded by that terror they obeyed, hanging spurs in their horses' flanks before they found stirrups, and the trio whirled down to the water.

"He's goin' home!" Rhues cried above the splashing. "That's our way out; we'll git him as we go 'long! We'll ride him down; he ain't got a gun! An' they'll find him out yonder with

LIFE, THE TROPHY

th' money belt on him! We —" He broke short with a laugh. "We could claim th' reward! Two fifty, dead 'r alive!"

Matson snarled something. Then, as their horses struggled up the far bank of the stream, completed it:

"—— with th' reward! What we want's a get-away!"

"We're on our way now," growled Rhues, and lashed his pony viciously with the ends of his bridle reins.

Knee to knee they raced, the ponies stretching their heads far out in efforts to cover that light ribbon of road which clove the cloudlike sage brush and ate up the distance between their position and that scudding blur ahead. Each had his gun drawn and held high in the right hand ready for use; each, with eyes only for that before them, with minds only for speed — and quick speculation on what might happen should they fail.

The creak of leather, the sharp batter of hoofs, the rattle of pebbles as they were thrown out against the rocks, the excited breathing of horses: A race, with human life the trophy!

And VB, looking back, saw. With set teeth he leaned still lower over the Captain's neck in spite of the raging the posture set up in his torn breast. No will of his had directed the stallion in that flight northward. His unexpected dash through the barn door, the quick recognition of the point they had scored, the sharp pang which came when VB realized the fact that the horse's break for home had cut him off from help that might have remained in Ranger, left the wounded man in a swirl of confused impressions.

Behind all the jumble was the big urge to reach that place which had been the only true haven of his experience. He felt a glimmer of solace when he sensed that he was going home which quite neutralized the terror that the glance at those oncoming riders provoked. The comfort inculcated by the idea grew into clear thinking; from there on into the status of an obsession. He was going home! He was on the way, with that mighty beast under him! He raised more of his weight to the stirrups and laid a reassuring hand on the snapping shoulder of his horse.

And on his trail rode the merciless three, their eyes following the bending course of the road, hat-brims now blown back against the crowns, now down over their eyes in the rush through the night. Rhues rode a quarter of a length ahead of the others, and his automatic was raised higher than were their gun-hands. Now and then one of the trio spoke sharply to his horse and grunted as he raked with a spur, but for the greater part of the time they did not lift their voices above the thunder of the race. They knew what must happen; they held their own, and waited!

"Go, boy, go!" whispered VB. "We'll run their legs off; they'll never get in range!"

The Captain held an attentive ear backward a moment, then shot it forward, watching the road, holding his rolling, space-eating stride. VB turned his head and again looked back. They were still there! No nearer — but he had not shaken them off. Two, perhaps three, miles had been covered and they hung by him, just within sight, just beyond that point where they might fire with an even chance of certainty. He pressed his arm against his burning breast, crowding the treasured money belt tighter against the wound. Somehow, it seemed to dull the torment, and for minutes he held the pressure constant, still lifted to supreme heights of endeavor and ability to withstand suffering by the rage that had welled up from his depths as he stood back in the shadow of the cabin and had the suspicion of how and why Kelly had met death become certainty.

Another mile, and he turned to look back again. They still hung there, making a blur in the moonlight, fanciful, half floating, but he knew they were real, knew that they hammered their way through the night with lust for his life!

"Captain!" he cried, apprehension rising. "Go it, boy; go it!"

He pressed a spur lightly against his side and felt the great beast quiver between strides. The pace quickened a trifle, but VB saw that the ears were no longer held steadily to the fore, that the head ducked with each leap forward as he had never seen it duck before. And as the thought with its killing remorse thundered into his intelligence, VB sat erect in the saddle with a gasp and a movement which staggered the running animal that bore him.

The Captain's strength had been drained! For twenty strides VB sat there, inert, a dead weight, while grief came into his throat, into his vision, deadening his mind. In all that melodrama which began when he stared through the saloon door and saw Rhues standing in the moonlight, gun ready, the reason for his presence in Ranger, the history of the earlier night, had been obliterated for the time being. Now, as he felt the beast under him labor, heard his heavy breathing, saw the froth on his lips, it all came back to Young VB.

"Oh, Captain!" he wailed, leaning forward again, eyes burning, throat choking.

And for a long time he rode as though unable to do else but hold his position over the fork of the saddle.

He was stunned, beaten down by poignant remorse. The Captain had made the long ride from Jed's to Ranger at a killing pace. VB remembered acutely now that the stallion had staggered as he emerged from Clear River and came into view of the saloon lights. And he had been there how long? An hour of poker, perhaps; an hour more at the outside. Two hours for the horse to regain the strength that had been taken from him in that cruel ride — a ride taken to satisfy the viciousness which made VB a man uncertain of himself!

The Captain had been wasted! He had gone, as had VB's heart and mind, to be a sacrifice for hideous gods! In an hour of weakness he had been offered, had been given gladly, and without thought of his value! For had not VB gloried in that ride to Ranger? Had it not been the end of all things for him? An end for which he was thankful? Had it not been all conscious, witting, planned? It had — and it had not been worth the candle!

The boy moaned aloud and wound his fingers in the flapping mane.

"Captain!" he cried. "It was all wrong — all false! I threw you away an hour ago, and now — you're *life* to me! Oh, boy, will you forgive? Can you?"

No fear of death tapped the wells of his grief. There was only sorrow for his wasting of that great animal, that splendid spirit, that clean strength!

After a moment he sobbed: "You can't do anything else but go on, boy! You're that sort! You'll go, then I'll go; anyhow, it will be together!"

And the great beast, blowing froth from his lips, struggled on, while from behind came the sounds of other running horses — perhaps a trifle nearer.

CHAPTER XXIV

Victory

THE road writhed on through the sage brush sixteen miles from Ranger before it branched. Then to the right ran the S Bar S route, while straight on it headed into Jed's ranch, and the left-hand course, shooting away from the others behind a long, rocky point, followed Sand Creek up to the cluster of buildings which marked the domicile of Dick Worth.

It was more than halfway. The Captain, now trotting heavily, now breaking once more into a floundering gallop, passed the first fork, that leading toward Worth's. With a gulp of relief VB saw that the moon hung low in the west — so low that the road home would be in the shadow of the point, which seemed to come down purposely to split the highway. He might then find refuge in darkness somewhere. He must have refuge!

At the tenth mile he had suspected, now he knew, that it would be impossible to stand off his pursuers clear to the ranch, and there were no habitations between him and Jed's.

"They have n't gained on you, boy!" he cried as he made out the distinct outlines of the point. "They're right where they were at the start!

No other horse in the world could have done it; not even you should be asked to do it — but — out —"

He choked back the sob that fought to come. He knew he must concentrate his last energy, now. If he came through there would be time to think of his crime against the Captain! But now — Futures depend on lives. His life dangled in the balance, and he wanted it, as men can want life only when they feel it slipping.

Back there three men raked the streaming sides of their ponies with vicious spurs.

"He can't make it!" Rhues swore. "Th' black's quittin' now! If he gits away, what chance we got? We got to git him! It'll give us th' last chance!"

"We're killin' our horses," growled Matson.

And Julio, a length behind, flogged his pinto mercilessly.

No craving for VB's life prompted Rhues now. He must go on for the sake of his own safety. He and those other two had all to gain and nothing to lose. If they could drop the man ahead it would be possible to skirt the ranches, catch fresh horses, and make on toward Wyoming. But let VB gain shelter with Jed or any one else, and a posse would be on their trail before they could be beyond reach.

No, there could be no turning back! They had made their bet; now they must back it with the whole stack. And before them — that blot in the moonlight — a wounded, suffering man cried aloud to the horse that moved so heavily under him.

"Make it to the point, Captain!" he begged. "Just there! It'll be dark! Only a little faster, boy!"

The stallion grunted under the stress of his effort, moving for the moment with less uncertainty, with a jot more speed.

They crawled up to the point and followed the bend of the road as it led into the dimness of the gulch. Across the way, far to the right, moonlight fell on the cliffs, but where the road hung close to the rise at the left all was in shadow.

To VB, entering the murk was like plunging from the heat of glaring day to the cool of a forest.

The men behind him would be forced to come twice as close before they could make firing effective. Then, when he reached the ranch —

He threw out an arm in a gesture of utter hopelessness. Reach the ranch? He laughed aloud, mocking his own guilelessness. He had come only a little more than half the distance now, and Captain could scarcely be held at a trot. Three miles, possibly five, he might last, and then his rider would have to face his pursuers with empty hands.

His was the very epitome of despair. A weaker man would have quit then, would have let the stallion flounder to his finish, would have waited submissively for Rhues to come and shoot him down.

But VB possessed the strength of his desperation.

Rhues might get him now, as he had tried to get him twice before, but he would get him by fighting. Not wholly for himself did the boy think, but for the likable, friendly Kelly, who had died there in his blankets without warning. If he could rid men of the menace which Rhues represented he would have done service, and the life of those last months had implanted within him the will to be of use — though, a few hours back, he might have thought it all a delusion.

So VB was alert with the acute alertness of mind which is given to humans when forced to fight to preserve life — when everything, the buried subconscious impulses, the forgotten, tucked-away memories, are in the fore, crying to help. Abandoning hope of reaching Jed's, he turned all his physical force, even, into the mental effort to seek a way out; fought his way to clarified thought, fought his way into logic. He could not go on much longer; there was no such thing as turning back, for he could hear them, nearer now! He could hear the click of pebbles as his pursuers' horses sent them scattering, and a pebble click will not travel far. Ahead — weakening muscles; behind — guns ready; to the right — moonlight; to the left —

The bridle rein drew across the Captain's lathered neck. The big beast swung to the left, out of the road, crashed through the brush, and lunged against the rise of rocks.

The horse seemed to sense the fact that this was the one remaining chance, the last possibility left in their bag of tricks. He picked his way up among the ragged bowlders and spiked brush with a quickness of movement that told of the breaking through into those reservoirs of strength which are held in man and beast until a last hope is found.

VB went suddenly faint. The loss of blood, the pain, the stress of nervous thought, the knowing that his full hand was on the table, caused him to reel dizzily in the saddle. He made no pretense of guiding the Captain. He merely sagged forward and felt the horse lunge and plunge and climb with him, heard the rasping breath that seemed to come from a torn throat.

Below and behind, the trailers swept from moonlight into shadow, horses wallowing as though that hard road were in deep mud, so great was the race that the stallion, spent though he might be, had given them. Rhues was ahead, revolver held higher than before, Matson's pony at his flank and Julio a dozen lengths behind. Bridle reins, knotted, hung loosely on their horses' necks; the three left hands rose and fell and quirts swished viciously through the night air.

"We got to close in!" Rhues cried. "We'll have him 'n a mile!"

And he called down on the heads of the horses awful imprecations for their weakness.

On into the darkness they stormed, Julio

trailing. And when Rhues had passed by fifty yards the point where the Captain had turned to take the steep climb the Mexican opened his throat in a cry, half of fright, half of exultation.

The Captain, almost at the end of his climb, leaping from rise to rise, had missed his footing. The soft earth slid as he jumped for a ledge of rock, and the front feet, coming down on the smooth surface in frantic clawing to prevent a fall, sent fire streaming from their shoes. In the darkness Julio had seen the orange sparks. At his cry the others set their ponies back on haunches and, following the Mexican, who now led, cursing VB and their weakening mounts, they commenced the climb. VB knew. The flash from the stallion's feet had roused him; he heard the shout; he knew what must follow. He gave no heed to the bullet which bored the air above him as he was silhouetted for the instant against moonlit space before he commenced the drop to the road leading up Sand Creek.

Where now? With a sigh which ended in a quick choking, as though he were through, ready to give up this ghost of a chance, ready to quit struggling on, the Captain dropped from the last little rim and turned into the road. Not on ahead — into that void where they could ride him down. Not back toward Ranger, for it was impossibly far. Where then? What was there? Sand Creek! And up Sand Creek was Dick Worth's!

VB caught his breath in a sob. It was the one

goal open to him, though the odds were crushing. He pressed the money belt tightly. Dick Worth was the man who should have that — Dick Worth, deputy sheriff! He lifted his voice and cried aloud the name of the deputy.

To the north once more the Captain headed, and with no word from VB took up the floundering way again. The boy looked behind and saw the others commence the drop down the moonlit point — saw one of the blurs slump quickly and heard a man scream. Then he leaned low on the stallion and talked to the horse as he would talk to a child who could pilot him to safety.

Behind him, along the road, came the blot again, now, however, smaller. VB did not know that it was Julio who had fallen, but he knew with a fierce delight that the Captain, running on his bare spirit, had killed off one of the pursuers!

The boy grew hysterical. He chattered to the stallion, knowing nothing of the words he uttered. At times his lips moved but uttered no sound. Continually his hands sought his breast. He knew from the dampness that crept down his side, on down into the trouser leg, that the wound still bled, that his life was running out through the gash.

Through the clamoring of his heart a familiar ache came into his throat, and the boy lifted his voice into the night with a rant of rage, of self-denunciation.

"Oh, Captain! You were the price!" he moaned.

But still he wanted — just one drink! Not to satisfy that craving now, but to keep him alive, a legitimate use for stimulant.

The stallion ceased pretense of galloping. Now and then he even dropped from his uncertain trotting to a walk.

VB, watching behind, could just make out those other travelers in the light of the low-hanging moon which seemed to balance on the ragged horizon and linger for sight of the finish of this grim drama worked out in the lonely stretches. As the horse stumbled more and more frequently under him VB knew that those who pressed him were coming closer. Then a flash of flame and a bullet spattered itself against a rock ahead and to the right.

"They're closer, Captain!" he muttered grimly. "The game's going against us — against you. I'm too much of a burden — too much weight."

His mind seized upon the aimless words. The suddenness of his shifting in the saddle made the stallion stagger, for VB's whole weight went into the right stirrup. He drew the other up with fiendish tinges shooting through his breast and tore at the cinch. It came loose. The saddle turned. VB flung his arms about the Captain's neck and kicked it from under him.

"Fifty pounds gone!" he muttered triumphantly, and the horse tossed his head.

quickening the trot, trying once again the heavy gallop.

VB could hear the horse breathing through his mouth. He looked down and saw that the long tongue flopped from the lips with every movement of the fine head. Tears came to his eyes as he caressed the Captain's withers frantically.

"Can I do more, boy?" he asked in a strained voice. "Can I do more?"

It was as though he pleaded with a dying human.

"Yes, I can do more!" he cried a moment later in answer to his own question. "You've given your whole to me; now I'll give you back your freedom, make you as free as you were the day I took you. I'll strip you, boy!"

He reached far out along the neck, drawing his weight up on the withers, and loosed the head-stall. The bridle fell into the road and the Captain ran naked! And, as though to show his gratitude, the horse shook his head groggily and reeled on in his crazy progress.

A half mile farther on the Captain fell. VB went down heavily and mounted the waiting horse again in a daze — from which he was roused by the fresh gushing on his breast. Another shot from behind — then two close together.

Dawn was coming. He looked around vaguely. The moon was slipping away. Perhaps yet it would be in at the finish. The shimmering light of new day was taking from objects their ghostly quality; making them real. The men behind could see VB — and they were firing!

The boy said no word to the Captain. He merely clamped his knees tighter and leaned lower on his neck. He had ceased to think, ceased to struggle. His trust, his life, was in the shaking legs of the animal he rode, whose sweat soaked through his clothing to mingle with the blood there.

The stallion breathed in great moaning sobs, as though his heart were bursting, as though his lungs were raw and bleeding. He reeled from side to side crazily. Now and then he ran out of the road and floundered blindly back. His head hung low, almost to his knees, and swung from side to side with each step, and at intervals he raised it as though it were a great weight, to gasp — and to sob!

From behind, bullets. Rhues and Matson fired grimly. They had ceased to lash their ponies, for it was useless. The beasts were beyond giving better service in return for punishment. Their sides dripped blood, but they were beyond suffering. Handicapped as he had been, the Captain had held them off, almost stride for stride.

Better light now, but their shooting could not hope to find a mark except through chance. They cursed in glad snarls as they saw the stallion reel, sink to his knees; then snarled again as they saw him recover and go on at his drunken trot.

Before VB's eyes floated a blotch of color. It was golden, a diffused light that comforted him; that, for some incomprehensible reason, was soothing to the senses. It eased the wound, too, and put new strength in his heart so that he could feel the warm blood seeping slowly into his numb arms and hands and fingers. He smiled foolishly and hugged the Captain's neck as the horse reeled along. Oh, it was a glorious color! He remembered the day he had seen a little patch of it scudding along the roadway in the sunshine. Why, it had seemed like concentrated sunshine itself.

"Gail," he murmured. "It was you — I didn't want to put — that mark — on you!"

The nature of that color became clear to him and he roused himself. It was a light — a light in a window — the window of a ranch house — Dick Worth's ranch house!

Bullets had ceased to zip and sing and spatter. He did not turn to see what had become of his pursuers, for he was capable of only one thought at a time.

"Dick Worth! Dick Worth!" he screamed.

Then he looked behind. Away to the left he saw two riders pushing through the dawn, détouring. And he laughed, almost gayly.

Another blotch of light, a bigger one, showed in the young day. It was an opened door, and a deep chest gave forth an answer to his cry. Dick Worth stepped from the threshold of his home and ran to the gate to see better this crazy figure which lurched toward him. It was a man on foot, hatless, his face gray like the sky above, hair tousled, eyes glowing red. He stumbled to the fence and leaned there for support, holding something forward, something limp and bloodstained.

"Dick — it's Kelly's money belt — Rhues — he killed him — He shot me — he's got the money — on him — he's swinging off west — two of 'em — Their horses are — all in — He — he shot Kelly because — I wouldn't take — a drink — he — and I need — a — drink —"

He slumped down against the fence.

After an uncertain age VB swam back from that mental vacuity to reality. He saw, first, that the Captain was beside him, standing there breathing loudly, eyes closed, sobbing low at every heave of his lungs.

A quavering moan made its way to the boy's throat and he moved over, reaching out groping arms for the stallion's lowered head.

"Captain!" he moaned. "Oh, boy — it was our last ride — I can never — ask you to carry me — again."

He hugged the face closer to his.

Then he heard a man's voice saying:

"Here, VB, take this — it'll brace you up!"

He turned his face slowly, for the strength that remained was far from certain. His wound was on fire, every nerve of his body laid bare. His will to do began and ended with wanting to hold that horse's head close. He was as a child, stripped of every effect that the experiences of his life could have had. He was weak, broken, unwittingly searching for a way back to strength.

He turned his head halfway and beheld the man stooping beside him who held in his hands a bottle, uncorked, and from it came a strong odor.

The boy dilated his nostrils and drew great breaths laden with the fumes of the stuff. A new life came into his eyes. They shone, they sparkled. Activity came to those bare nerves, and they raised their demands.

He opened his mouth and let the odor he inhaled play across that place in his throat. The smell went on out through his arteries, through his veins, along the nerves to the ends of his being, to the core of his soul! He was down, down in the depths, his very ego crying for the stimulant, for something to help it come back.

He coaxed along that yearning, let it rise to its fullest. Then he raised his eyes to meet the concerned gaze of the other man. And the man saw in those eyes a look that made him sway back, that made him open his lips in surprise.

"To hell with that stuff!" the boy screamed. "To hell with it! To hell — *to hell!* It belongs there! It — it killed the Captain!"

Tears came with the sobs, and strength to

the arms that held the stallion's head; strength that surged through his entire body, stilling those nerves, throttling the crying of his throat. For VB had gone down to his test, his real ordeal, and had found himself not wanting.

CHAPTER XXV

"The Light!"

JED AVERY sat alone. It was night, a moonlight night in Colorado, the whole world bathed in a cold radiance that conduces to dreams and fantasies.

But as he sat alone Jed's mind wove no light reveries. Far from it, indeed. He was sodden in spirit, weakened in nerve.

He rested his body on the edge of a chair seat and leaned far forward, elbows on his knees. His fingers twined continually, and on occasion one fist hammered the palm of the other hand.

"You old fool!" he whispered. "You old fool! Now, if he's gone —"

For twenty-four hours he had not dared frame the words.

He lifted his eyes to the window, and against the moonlight stood a bottle, its outlines distorted by incrustings of tallow. No candle was in its neck. There was only the bottle.

After a time the old man got up and paced the floor, three steps each way from the splotch of moonlight that came through the window. He had been walking that way for a night and a day — and now it was another night.

While it was daylight he had walked outside,

eyes ever on the road, hoping, fearing. And no one had come! Now, as the night wore on and the boy did not return, Jed's condition bordered on distraction.

His pacing became faster and more fast. He lengthened the limits of his walk to those of the room, and finally in desperation jerked open the door to walk outside.

But he did not leave the threshold. Two figures, a man and a horse, coming up the road held him as though robbed of the will to move. He stood and stared, breathing irregularly. The man, who walked ahead, made his way slowly toward the gate. He was followed by the horse, followed as a dog might follow, for not so much as a strap was on the animal. The man's movements were painful, those of the horse deliberate.

Jed knew both those figures too well to be mistaken, even though his sight dimmed.

He wanted to cry out, but dared not. One question alone crowded to get past his teeth. The answer would mean supremest joy or sorrow. Fear of the latter held him mute.

The man unfastened the gate and let it swing open. "Come, boy," he said gently, and the big animal stepped inside.

With the same slow movements again, the man closed the bars.

Jed stood silent. A coyote high on the hills lifted his voice in a thin yapping, and the sound made Old VB shiver.

The boy came slowly toward the house. He saw Jed, but gave no sign, nor did the old man move. He stood there, eyes on the other in a misted stare, and VB stopped before him, putting a hand against the wall for support.

Then came the question, popping its way through unwilling, tight lips:

"Shall I light th' candle, Young VB?"

His voice was shrill, strained, vibrant with anxiety. But VB did not answer — merely lifted a hand to his hot head.

"VB, when you left last night th' candle dropped down into th' bottle an' went out. I did n't dare light a new one to-night —" His voice broke, and he paused a moment. "I did n't dare light it until I knowed. I've been settin' in th' dark here, thinkin' things — tryin' not to think dark things."

One hand went halfway to his mouth in fear as he waited for the other to answer. VB put a hand on Jed's shoulder, and the old man clamped his cold fingers over it desperately.

"Yes, Jed — light it," he said huskily. Then he raised his head and looked at the old man with a half smile. "Light it, Jed. Let it burn on and on, just for the sake of being bright. But *we* — we don't need it any more. Not for the old reason, Jed."

The cold hand twitched as it gripped the hot one.

"Not for the old reason, Jed," VB continued. "There's a bigger, better, truer light burning now. It won't slip into the bottle; it can't be blown out. It didn't waver when the true crisis came. It'll always burn; it won't slip down into the bottle. It's — it's the real thing."

He staggered forward, and Jed caught him, sobbing like a woman, a happy woman.

They had the whole story over then by the light of a fresh candle.

When Jed started forward with a cry at the recital of the shooting VB pushed him off.

"It's only a flesh wound; it don't matter — much. Mrs. Worth dressed it, and I'm all right. It's the Captain I want to tell about — the Captain, Jed!"

And he told it all, in short, choking sentences, stripping his soul naked for the little rancher. He did not spare himself, not one lone lash. He ended, crushed and bleeding before the eyes of his friend. After a pause he straightened back in his chair, the new fire in his eyes, the fire the man at Worth's had seen when he offered drink.

"But I've got to make it up to the Captain now," he said with a wild little laugh. "I've got to go on. He gave me the chance. He took me into blackness, into the test I needed, and brought me back to light. I've got to be a man, Jed — a man —"

And throughout the night Jed Avery tended the wound and watched and muttered — with joy in his heart.

Morning came, with quieted nerves for VB. He lay in the bunk, weak, immobile.

Jed came in from tending the horses.

"He did n't bleed, did he, VB?"

"No."

"It ain't what you thought, sonny. It ain't bad. Give him a rest an' he'll be better'n ever. Why, he's out there now, head up, whisperin' for you! You can't break a spirit like his unless you tear his vitals out!"

VB smiled, and the smile swelled to a laugh.

"Oh, Jed, it makes me so happy! But it won't be as it was. I can never let him carry me again."

The old man turned on the boy a puzzled look.

"What you goin' to do with him, VB — turn him loose again?"

"Not that, Jed; he would n't be happy. He'll never carry me again, but perhaps — perhaps he could carry a light rider — a girl — a woman."

And from Jed: "Oh-o-o-o!"

An interval of silence.

"That is," muttered VB, "if she'll take him, and —"

"Would you want him away from you?" the old man insisted.

"Oh, I hope it won't be that, Jed! I hope not — but I want her to — You understand. Jed? You understand?"

The other nodded his head, a look of grave tenderness in the old eyes.

"Then — then, Jed, I'm all right. I can get along alone. Would you mind riding over and — asking her if she'd come —

"You see, Jed, I know now. I did n't before — I'm sure it's worth the candle — and there'll be no more darkness; no lasting night for her if —"

Jed walked slowly out into the other room and picked up his spurs. VB heard him strap them on, heard his boots stamp across the floor and stop.

"I'd go, VB, but it ain't necessary."

The boy raised his head, and to his ears came the bellow of a high-powered motor, the sound growing more distinct with each passing second.

"Lord, how that woman's drivin'!" Jed cried. "Lordy!" And he ran from the house.

The bellow of the motor rose to a sound like batteries of Gatlings in action; then came the wail of brakes.

With a pulsing thrill VB heard her voice upraised — with such a thrill that he did not catch the dread in her tone as she questioned Jed.

She came to him swiftly, eyes dimmed with tears, without words, and knelt by his bunk, hands clasped about his head. For many minutes they were so, VB gripping her fine, firm forearms. Then she raised her face high.

"And you would n't let me help?" she asked querulously.

He looked at her long and soberly, and took both her hands in his.

"It was the one place you couldn't help," he muttered. "It was that sort — my love, I mean. I had to know; had to know that I wouldn't put a hateful mark on you by loving. I had to know that. Don't you see?"

She moved closer and came between him and the sunshine that poured through the open door. The glorious light was caught by her hair and thrown, it seemed, to the veriest corners of the dingy little room.

"The light!" he cried.

She settled against him, her lips on his, and clung so. From outside came the shrilling call of the Captain. VB crushed her closer.

CHAPTER XXVI

TO THE VICTOR

UP the flagged walk to the house of chill. white stone overlooking the North River went a messenger, and through the imposing front portal he handed a letter, hidden away in a sheaf of others. A modest-appearing letter; indeed, perhaps something less than modest; possibly humble, for its corners were crumpled and its edges frayed. Yet, of all the packages handed him, Daniel Lenox, alone at his breakfast, singled it out for the earliest attention.

And what he read was this:

DEAR FATHER:

In my last letter—written ten years ago, it seems—I promised to tell you my whereabouts when I had achieved certain ends. I now write to tell you that I am at the Thorpe Ranch, one hundred and thirty miles northwest of Colt, Colorado, the nearest railroad point.

I can inform you of this now because I have won my fight against the thing which would have stripped me of my manhood. And I want to make clear the point that it was you, father, who showed me the way, who made me realize to what depths I had gone.

I am very humble, for I know the powers that rule men.

When I left New York there was little in me to

interest you, but I am making bold enough to tell you of the greatest thing in my life. I have won the love of a good woman. We are to be married here the twentieth, and some day I will want to bring her East with me. I hope you will want to see her.

Your son,
Danny.

While the hand of the big clock made a quarter circle the man sat inert in his chair; limp, weak in body, spirit, and mind, whipped by the bitterest lashes that human mind can conjure. Then he raised his chin from his breast and rested his head against the back of the chair, while his hands hung loose at his sides.

His lips moved. "Hope — you will want to see her," he repeated in a whisper.

A pause, and again words:

"He would n't even ask me — would n't dream I wanted to — be there!"

An old man, you would have said, old and broken. The snap, the precision that had been his outstanding characteristic, was gone. But not for long. The change came before the whispering had well died; the lines of purpose, of decision, returned to his face, his arms ceased to hang limp, the look in the eyes — none the less warm — became definite, focused.

Suddenly Daniel Lenox sat erect and raised the letter to the light once more.

"The twentieth!" he muttered. "And this is —"

Another train fumed at the distances, left

cities behind, and crawled on across prairies to mountain ranges. As it progressed, dispatchers, one after another, sat farther forward in their chairs and the alert keenness of their expression grew a trifle sharper. For the Lenox Special, New York to Colt, Colorado, invited disaster with every mile of its frantic rush across country. Freights, passenger trains, even the widely advertised limiteds, edged off the tracks to let it shriek on unhampered.

In the swaying private car sat the man who had caused all this disarray of otherwise neat schedules. At regular, short intervals his hand traveled to watch-pocket and his blue eyes scrutinized the dial of his timepiece as though to detect a lie in the sharp, frank characters. In the other hand, much of the time, were held sheets of limp paper. They had been folded and smoothed out again so many times and, though he was an old man and one who thought mostly in figures, fondled so much, that the ink on them 'was all but obliterated in places.

He read and reread what was written there as the train tore over the miles, and as he read the great warmth came back to his eyes. With it, at times, a fear came. When fear was there, he tugged at his watch again.

Up grades, through cañons, the special roared its way. At every stop telegrams zitted ahead, and hours before the train was due an automobile waited by the depot platform at Colt.

Daniel Lenox heeded not the enthusiastic trainmen who held watches and calculated the broken record as brakes screamed down and the race by rail ended. Bag in hand, he strode across the cinder platform and entered the waiting automobile, without a single glance for the group that looked at him wonderingly.

"You know the way to the Thorpe Ranch?" he asked the driver of the car.

"Like a book!"

"Can you drive all night?"

"I can."

"Good! We must be there as early to-morrow as possible."

And ten minutes before noon the next day the heavy-eyed driver threw out his clutch and slowed the car to a stop before the S Bar S ranch house. Saddled horses were there, a score of them standing with bridle reins down. Sounds of lifted voices came from the house, quickly lulled as an exclamation turned attention on the arrival.

From the ample door came a figure — tall and lean, well poised, shoulders square, feet firm on the ground. Pale, true, but surely returning strength was evidenced in his very bearing. VB's lips moved. His father, halfway to him, stopped.

"Dad!"

"Am I on time?" queried the older man.

"*Dad!*"

With a cry the boy was up on him, grasping both hands in his.

"I didn't — dare hope you'd want — Dad, it makes me so —"

The other looked almost fiercely into the boy's face, clinging to the hands that clutched his, shaking them tremblingly now and then. The penetrating blue eyes searched out every line in the boy's countenance, and the look in them grew to be such as VB had never seen before.

"Did you think I'd stay back there in New York and let you do all this alone? Did you think I would n't come on, in time if I could, and tell you how ashamed I am to have ever doubted you, my own blood, how mean a thing was that which I thought was faith?"

His gaze went from VB to Gail, coming toward him clad all in simple white, flushing slightly as she extended her hand. He turned to her, took the hand, and looked deep into her big eyes. He tried to speak, but words would not come and he shook his head to drive back the choking emotion.

"Bless you!" he finally muttered. "Bless you both. You're a man — Danny. And you —"

His voice failed again and he could only remain mute, stroking the girl's hand.

Then Jed came up and greeted the newcomer silently, a bit grimly, as though he had just forgiven him something.

"Come over here, you three," said VB, and led them over to where two horses stood together

One was the bay the boy had ridden that afternoon he charged down the ridge to make the great stallion his, and beside him, towering, head up, alert, regally self-conscious, stood the Captain. The bay bore VB's saddle. On the Captain's back perched one of smaller tree, silver mounted and hand tooled, with stirrups that were much too short for a man.

They looked the great horse over silently, moving about him slowly, and Danny pointed out his fine physical qualities to his father. A rattling of wheels attracted them and they looked up to see a team of free-stepping horses swing toward them, drawing a light buckboard. The vehicle stopped and from it stepped a man in the clothing of a clergyman.

"He's here, VB," Jed muttered. "To be sure, an' he's got his rope down, too. Th' iron's hot; th' corral gate's open and he's goin' to head you in. 'T ain't often you see such a pair of high-strung critters goin' in so plumb docile, Mister Lenox!"

And from the corner of his eye he saw the man beside him wipe his hand across his cheek, as though to brush something away.

The Captain pawed the ground sharply. Then he lifted his head high, drew a great breath, and peered steadily off toward the distant ridges, eagerly, confidently, as though he knew that much waited — out yonder.